IT'S
NOT AS BAD
AS
IT SEEMS

A Thinking Straight
Approach to Happiness

Memphis • Castle Books • Memphis

P.O. Box 17262   Memphis, TN   38187

ACKNOWLEDGEMENTS

Like the old saying goes, "There is nothing new under the sun." That is true of this book as well. The ideas presented in this book are based on Rational-Emotive Therapy developed by Albert Ellis, Ph.D. Dr. Ellis and many other cognitive behavior therapists have greatly influenced my personal and professional growth over the years and deserve the credit for the ideas presented in this book. Some of those who have been most instrumental in my professional development include Dr. Ray DiGiuseppe and Dr. Ellis as well as many other supervisors and staff members at the Institute for Rational-Emotive Therapy in New York. Some of the information presented is also based on material developed by Dr. Aaron Beck, Dr. David Burns, and Dr. Maxie Maultsby.

Most of the credit for this book goes to the clients with whom I have worked over the years since 1977. I learn from these individuals every day, and it was with their encouragement that I actually decided to pursue this project.

I would like to thank Dr. Ellis for his willingness to review an earlier draft of this book. His comments and suggestions were extremely helpful.

Thanks also to Nancy (aka Mac) McGovern who deserves the credit for her fine editing, proofreading, and patient typing of the various drafts. Many thanks to Charles Goodman and Castle Books for the encouragement and assistance necessary for the publication of this book; and thanks to Sylvia Rose for her graphics.

My wife Christy Nottingham gets the credit for tolerating my irrational thinking while working on this book, and more importantly, deserves my deepest appreciation for her support and encouragement.

My mother and father get a special thanks for having been pretty darn rational thinkers and having influenced me in many positive and healthy ways.

INTRODUCTION

Several years ago, I began to think about how nice it would be if there was a book or manual that summarized many of the topics that I discussed with my clients in therapy.

One of my desires was to let people know that while we all experience pain, disappointment, and suffering in various forms, we are not required to embrace and hold onto the suffering, which can cause serious emotional disturbances.

One of the unique aspects of being human is that we have choices. In this book, we will explore these choices and you will discover how you can increase your personal effectiveness, your psychological wellness, and your happiness by applying the principles of an effective and efficient form of therapy, one that is called Rational-Emotive Therapy.

This book is designed to get you, the reader, involved. It will be important to complete the homework assignments in order to learn the principles and techniques being presented. I often think that learning to apply the "thinking-straight approach" is much like learning a foreign language. At first, we may think it's impossible, but with persistent work and practice, what once seemed impossible becomes a reality.

As you read, you will find yourself identifying with some of the problems. However, the book is not to take the place of counseling or therapy. If you begin to think that you have some of the problems described, I encourage you to call a therapist, make an appointment, and discuss them. The decision to seek counseling or therapy is a sign of strength that deserves our congratulations.

I want to make it clear that the therapy sessions included in this book were not actual verbatim sessions. In these chapters, I have created fictional examples that can be useful to the reader. No material from any actual therapy session has been used. Many clients who read early drafts of this book commented that they found themselves being described in a certain chapter, even though I hadn't known them at the time I wrote that chapter! This illustrated that, while we are all unique, we also share many universal characteristics and problems. As you recognize that you may share some of the problems presented in this book, keep in mind that the book is about solutions, not problems.

After you read the book, let me hear from you. Drop me a line. Let me know what you thought was helpful in the book, what you didn't like so well, and include any suggestions you may have. My office mailing address is 7516 Enterprise Avenue, Suite 1, Germantown, TN, 38138.

Library of Congress Catalog
Card Number 92-075828

Published by Castle Books, Inc.
P. O. Box 17262
Memphis, Tennessee
38138

ISBN 0 916693 16 3

Printed in the United States of America

Contents

CHAPTER ONE

Why Can't I Be Happy?

Your happiness is intertwined with your outlook on life.

-Anonymous

How many times have you heard that question, "Why can't I be happy?" How many times have you asked yourself that question?

It's asked by many of the people I've talked to over the years. It seems to be a fair question. Why can't we be happy?

I believe that there are some serious problems associated with our search for happiness. First, over the years, I have become increasingly convinced that as humans, we are not necessarily pre-wired for happiness (although some approaches to therapy suggest that if we are just left to our own devices, we can "self-actualize" and find happiness).

Second, we live in a world in which it is easy to develop bad habits that can get in our way of achieving a reasonable degree of happiness and contentment. We learn a lot of "if only's." If only we had a good job, a big house, a nice car, and lots of love, then (and maybe only then) we would be happy. We begin to compare ourselves to our friends, neighbors, even relative strangers, all of those people who seem to have "more" and therefore are better and "happier" than we are. We begin to believe that once we achieve what these people have achieved, then we will be happy.

So happiness, and our pursuit of it, becomes directly related to outside events, achievements, possessions, and other external factors. Therefore, all people who achieve their goals and who have nice cars, big houses, and terrific loving relationships are, of course, happy. Right?

Wrong!

Why isn't this true?

While a number of external factors do play a role in the human condition, such as economic conditions, environmental stressors, and physical health, the big piece of the puzzle that seems to pull it all together is "**outlook**."

Outlook

Let me use several examples. Stephen Covey, in his book, *The Seven Habits of Highly Effective People*[1] tells a story of a subway ride that he once took in New York City. A man with several young children got on and sat down beside Dr. Covey and closed his eyes. But the children were full of energy, running up and down the subway car, screaming, and pulling newspapers from passengers' hands. As this ruckus continued for some time, Covey found himself becoming increasingly irritated.

Stop for a minute and put yourself in Dr. Covey's place. Imagine that you've been working all day, you're tired, and you would like a little peace and quiet on your ride home. Imagine the screaming children running up and down the subway car, trying to pull your book or newspaper from your hands. How would you feel? Write down the feelings you might have in the space below:

Dr. Covey tells us that he finally turned to the gentleman and asked him if he would please do something to control his children. The man slowly opened his eyes and looked at Dr. Covey. "Oh, you're right," he said. "I guess I should do something about it. We just came from the hospital where their mother died about an hour ago. I don't know what to think, and I guess they don't know how to handle it, either."[2]

IT'S NOT AS BAD AS IT SEEMS

What do you think happened to Dr. Covey's feelings of irritation? Remember, the children are still running up and down the aisle, out of control. But he tells us that his feelings of irritation suddenly disappeared and were replaced with feelings of sympathy and compassion as he asked the gentleman how he might be able to help.

As you pictured this situation in your mind, and you learned of the death, did your feelings change? Why?

Outlook.

A second example of the importance of outlook is offered by Howard Young in a little book called, *A Rational Counseling Primer*.[3] He tells the story of two young children playing in the ocean (and I suggest imagining that these two children are identical twins, as close to being carbon copies as is possible), when suddenly a big wave comes in and knocks them both down. One child gets up, starts crying, and runs to his mother and father, quite frightened. The other twin gets up and laughs, staying in the water and waiting for another big wave to come along.

The "outside event" is the same. Both children are in the same water, both children get hit by the same wave, yet they react in very different ways.

Again, I suggest that you put yourself in this situation and imagine how you might react. Imagine that you're standing in the water, and imagine that there are lots of other people in the water with you. Suddenly you all get hit by a big wave. Would each of you react the same way? Why?

Outlook.

A final and more personal example. In order to be available to clients, I carry a beeper. One day I was leading group therapy, and my beeper went off. I looked down and was startled to see the emergency code on the beeper, instructing me to immediately call my office. All of a sudden, I felt myself tensing up, breathing more rapidly, and feeling quite uncomfortable. I immediately called my office, only to learn that a piece of furniture I had ordered some months before had arrived.

What do you think happened to my feelings of tension and discomfort? More importantly, what "caused" them in the first place? Was it hearing the beeper go off? Was it seeing the emergency code? And as the other people in the room also heard the beeper and learned from me that it was an emergency code, did each of them feel the same degree of discomfort and tension that I did? What made the difference?

Outlook.

In all of these situations, things happen and people react. But outlook affects their reactions. Dr. Covey feels irritation, but when he gets additional information, he feels compassion. The twins are knocked over by the same wave, yet react very differently. My beeper goes off, and I think that something bad has happened and begin to feel uncomfortable. These feelings and reactions are largely caused by the **outlook** and **attitude** of those involved.

Outlook, as well as belief, attitude, and self-talk, will play the most important roles in this book. You will learn that how you feel and react in a particular situation (and often, how "happy" you are) is not based on the external factors but is largely the result of how you think, what you believe, and what you tell yourself about that situation.

Of course, this is nothing new. The idea that happiness comes from within and is based on what we think rather than what we accomplish or what we own is taught in the Book of Proverbs (23:7), where we learn that as a person thinks, so he or she is. Epictetus, a philosopher in the First Century, wrote that people are not disturbed by things, but rather by the views they hold of these things. In Shakespeare's *Hamlet*, we read that *nothing* is either good nor bad, but thinking makes it so.

"Things" such as external events certainly play an important role in triggering our emotional reactions. But since we may have little control over these outside events, why not learn to control what we can - our outlook and thinking?

IT'S NOT AS BAD AS IT SEEMS

Oh, no! Is this going to be another book on "positive think-ing"? I certainly hope not. While it may help in some situations, I am not a big fan of positive thinking, but rather of rational, logical, and non-negative thinking. Positive thinking suggests that when bad things do indeed happen to us - and they will! - we should just "think positively" and simply "feel good" in order to cope with the situation. But when bad things happen to me, I don't want to necessarily feel good! Rather, I want to feel appropriately, even if this means feeling appropriately bad. When important people in my life have died, I've appreciated that I've been able to feel intensely sad and to appropriately mourn their deaths. I didn't want to feel good.

However, if my outlook about their deaths became intensely negative, my sadness might easily change to depression, which will certainly block my pursuit of happiness and effectiveness.

I think of therapy and counseling as education, and therefore in many ways, this book is going to be a textbook on the pursuit of happiness. Think of it as an independent study course in uncovering your own personal blocks to happiness. Think of it as an opportunity to develop skills that will increase the likelihood of creating reasonable happiness and contentment more of the time, skills that are necessary to handle stressful situations when they do happen.

Since this is independent study, there will be opportunities to answer some questions as you go through the chapters in this book and there will be **homework**. That's right, homework! This homework will be designed to keep you actively involved in this course. My experience has been that the more involved people are in their own pursuit of happiness, the more progress they make.

Suggested Homework for Chapter One:

Start today. Begin to keep a diary or journal in which you log those daily situations when you find yourself feeling an emotion quite strongly. You may find yourself feeling very angry, frustrated, anxious, or depressed. Or you may be feeling intensely happy, excited, or enthusiastic.

IT'S NOT AS BAD AS IT SEEMS

In your diary, pick up on each of these emotions, and answer the following four questions for each situation:

1. What is the feeling?

2. How strongly did you feel the emotion (on a scale of 0 to 10, with 0 being "not at all" and 10 being "the most extreme possible")?

3. What was going on immediately before you started feeling the emotion?

4. And finally, what was your "outlook" in this situation? You can begin to pick up on this outlook by asking yourself, "What was going through my mind right then when I had that feeling?"

As you read on, it will become easier and easier for you to pick up on your thoughts, beliefs, attitudes, and outlooks, but for now just do the best that you know how.

CHAPTER TWO

The ABC's of Thinking Straight

Remember, happiness doesn't depend upon who you are
or what you have; it depends solely upon what you think.

- Dale Carnegie

Do you remember being a young child and learning your ABC's? It was probably accomplished due to much practice and patience on the part of your parents and teachers. And finally armed with this new knowledge, you were able to read and write, and a whole new exciting world opened to you.

Now I would like to introduce you to an even more wonderful set of ABC's. By using this new knowledge, we can begin to understand not only why at times it seems that we can't be happy, but also and more importantly, how to create greater happiness and contentment in our lives.

When we look back, learning those early reading and writing skills may seem easy. They are simple skills, but as a child, it sure wasn't easy mastering them. Likewise, as you begin learning the new ABC's associated with thinking straight, they may sound simple and straightforward, but it won't be easy to apply them skillfully to our lives.

Often when we attempt to learn new skills and find the process somewhat difficult, our tendency is to throw up our hands and quit. As you begin to learn and apply the skills being presented in this book, you may also want to quit. Please, don't! Obviously, if you're reading this book, you've already learned one set of ABC's, which suggests to me that you can also learn the ABC's of thinking straight.

IT'S NOT AS BAD AS IT SEEMS

The ABC's of Thinking Straight

The ABC's that you will learn in this chapter were developed by Albert Ellis, Ph.D. When Dr. Ellis completed his Ph.D. in clinical psychology, he had learned about a type of therapy that emphasized spending a great deal of time listening to the client talk about his or her childhood, parents, and so on. While he was quite effective in applying this form of therapy, Dr. Ellis became increasingly dissatisfied with the inefficiency of this approach, particularly with the amount of time required for people to make important emotional and behavioral changes.

But rather than just be dissatisfied, Dr. Ellis did something of great importance. In 1955, he introduced **Rational-Emotive Therapy**, or **RET**. RET is a form of therapy that helps people to eliminate emotional upsetness and defeating actions and behaviors, and more importantly, to reach their goals and live more fulfilling, happier lives. Since 1955, research has supported the effectiveness of Rational-Emotive Therapy, and many people have benefitted from skills learned from RET. But let's move on to the ABC's of RET.

A :   Activators

Which brings us back to the ABC's of thinking straight. The **A** stands for **Activator**, or **Activating Event**. These activating events can be "bad" things that happen to us (such as illnesses, accidents, arguments, relationship breakups, or job losses) or in our world (such as floods, wars, or natural disasters). Or they can be "good" things (such as job promotions, marriages, or buying a new home).

In Chapter One, the activators were the screaming children on the subway, the big wave that knocked the children down, and the urgent message displayed on my beeper.

Most of the time it's easy to identify these activators because we can see, touch, feel, or otherwise confirm the existence of these outside events or experiences. However, activators don't have to be external. Activators can also be internal. They can be memories of good or bad things that have happened in the past, physical sensations, or even feelings. Activators can also be anticipated events or events that you <u>predict</u> or <u>forecast</u> will happen. For example, you may anticipate an argument with your boss or start to anticipate that something bad is going to happen.

B: Beliefs

In the RET approach to thinking straight and happiness, **B** stands for **Beliefs**. Beliefs are the "meat and potatoes" of happiness or unhappiness, contentment or misery. Fortunately, they are the part of our world over which we can gain more and more control.

Beliefs come in many forms, including thoughts, attitudes, self-statements, cognitions, and underlying assumptions. I like to think of beliefs as our general and specific outlook.

In Chapter One, Dr. Covey had no control over the screaming children, the twins had no control over the big wave, and I had no control over the message that was displayed on my beeper. But, we are able to control our "B" or beliefs in each of those situations, that is, that personal set of thoughts, attitudes, and assumptions that we each carry with us.

C: Consequences

C stands for **Consequences**, that is, the outcomes that occur as a result of our beliefs (B). Many types of consequences can occur as a result of our outlooks, beliefs, and attitudes, but they tend to be either **Emotional** (feeling) **Consequences** or **Behavioral** (action) **Consequences**.

Depending on our outlook, our **Emotional Consequences** can be healthy and appropriate (such as sadness, concern, regret, annoyance, disappointment, and irritation). Or they can be inappropriate, destructive, unhealthy, and defeating (such as depression, intense anger, anxiety, hostility, rage, self-pity, and strong frustration).

It is these unhealthy emotional responses that can certainly get in the way of achieving our goals, and it is these unhealthy emotional consequences that will most likely block our pursuit of happiness and contentment.

IT'S NOT AS BAD AS IT SEEMS

If we are human, and I assume we all are, we will always have emotions. The goal of thinking straight is not to become a robot or unemotional, but rather, to be able to have more healthy and appropriate emotions and, therefore, emotional consequences. Some people have learned to stuff their emotions. Some even believe that emotions are bad, that emotions are their enemies.

I like to think of our emotions and feelings as being friends and allies that provide us with important information. What are you feeling right now? Mad, sad, glad, scared, frustrated, or bad? What's happening inside your body from the neck down? How is your breathing? What is your pulse? Do you have tight feelings in your belly, or are you feeling relaxed?

These bodily sensations are often "early warning signals" that can help us get in touch with some of the emotional consequences that we may be experiencing.

So, one type of C that we have is an emotional consequence. But there is another type of consequence, too. These are the behaviors and reactions that go along with the emotions that we are feeling. We refer to these as the **Behavioral Consequences**. Usually, when we feel something, we respond to that feeling. We take action. We do, or decide not to do, something. These actions can be seen in many cases, such as kicking the helpless dog, throwing things, crying, yelling, storming out of the house, deliberately avoiding doing something, or staying to ourselves and avoiding other people.

Behavioral consequences, like emotional consequences, can be appropriate and enhancing, or inappropriate and defeating. For example, if we feel annoyed or irritated with a person who has mistreated us in some way, and we directly and assertively express our feelings to that person, we have felt and behaved appropriately, effectively, and enhancingly. However, if we feel extreme anger with this person, and begin shouting, throwing things, and hitting, our reactions are inappropriate and defeating (unless you consider spending time in jail self-enhancing!).

IT'S NOT AS BAD AS IT SEEMS

The **C** in the thinking straight approach to happiness may be thought of as the "bleep" that shows up on our psychological radar screen. If you were an air traffic controller and had the responsibility of monitoring radar screens, you would watch carefully for the bleeps to show up. However, if you were in the military, perhaps a soldier whose responsibility it was to monitor the screens for possible enemy intruders, and you suddenly saw a bleep on the screen, would you immediately push the panic button? Why not? Give some thought to that right now.

What did you come up with? Chances are you wouldn't push the button because you know that the bleep on the screen could represent many different situations. The bleep could be a friendly passenger airliner, a flock of birds, or merely atmospheric conditions. It would be necessary to get much more information in order to determine whether the bleep was friend or foe.

Likewise, it's helpful to have a way of determining whether our emotional and behavioral "bleeps" (consequences) are friend or foe. One rule of thumb might be to ask ourselves whether our consequences are helpful, healthy, enhancing, and effective. Are our feelings and actions helping us to reach our goals, improve our quality of life, and enjoy ourselves? Do they also serve to enhance and assist others and have a healthy impact on important relationships? That is, are our emotional and behavioral consequences other- and relationship-enhancing?

If I were to feel angry and yell at others, at some level I might believe that it was good that I "got my anger out." However, if my angry outburst has a strong negative impact on other people, or results in close friends avoiding me like the plague, then my emotional and behavioral consequences have been other- and relationship-defeating.

When I was a hippie in the 1960s and early '70s, the popular saying was, "If it feels good, do it." But what if it feels good, and we do it, but our actions are excessive, destructive, and defeating to self, others, and relationships? If this is the case, chances are our beliefs at point B are quite crooked, and an adjustment of these beliefs is necessary.

D: *Disputation*

What does it take to accomplish this belief and attitude adjustment? As you will see, much of the RET thinking straight approach to happiness focuses on the D of the new ABC's that you are learning. **D** stands for **Disputation** of those beliefs (that is, our attitudes, thoughts, and assumptions) that we have determined are unhealthy, destructive, and defeating. In other words, they are getting in the way of our happiness.

Disputation is one part of Rational-Emotive Therapy that sets it apart from many other types of therapy and counseling. Disputation is an active, creative, even exciting process. Disputation is the debating, challenging, and questioning of our unhealthy beliefs. Successful disputation helps us to not only temporarily "feel better," but also to get better, stay better, and keep moving in the right direction, down the path toward our long-term goals.

The **"Big D"** is disputation, but we also have **"Little D's"** that are very important. The first stands for **Detecting**. Think back to the radar screen, and those little "bleeps." You have to notice that there are bleeps on the radar screen before you can take any other action on them. Detecting represents that first step of noticing the bleeps. Before we can decide whether a belief is helpful or hurtful, we have to be able to detect what is going through our mind, what we are telling ourselves, and what that basic belief really is.

After detecting what the underlying belief is, we begin to develop a "camera's eye view" of ourselves in order to determine whether the accompanying behavioral consequences are enhancing or defeating to ourselves, others, or relationships. Dr. Maxie Maultsby developed a form of therapy related to RET called **Rational Behavior Therapy** or **RBT**, that emphasizes developing this camera's eye view or "camera check."[1]

Over the next few weeks, I want you to imagine that there is an internal video camera recording your every action. This camera is special because it records not only specific actions, but also magically records thoughts and statements going through your head. In this exercise, take a few minutes out of each hour, stop, and rewind your special video recorder. Now, play it back on a magical internal VCR.

Begin detecting your specific thoughts (beliefs) and accompanying feelings and actions (emotional and behavioral consequences) during situations in which you were feeling good, and not so good. Be very specific in describing these feelings and actions. If you were feeling angry or "got mad" (emotional consequence) what exactly did you do (behavioral consequence)?

Write down some of the thoughts, assumptions, and self-talk (beliefs) that your magical video camera recorded. Then look for clenched fists, rapid breathing, loud tone of voice, and other specific behaviors (behavioral consequences). Take some time right now and try it.

The activator or situation that immediately preceded by feelings and reactions was:

The feelings I had in this situation were:

My behaviors and actions were:

My beliefs, thoughts, assumptions, and self-talk were:

For example, while driving, my video camera might record me as I begin to tense up, breathe rapidly, make a fist, and blow the horn. It would also record thoughts such as, "How dare you cut me off!" "You don't know how to drive!" and "You shouldn't act so stupidly!"

IT'S NOT AS BAD AS IT SEEMS

Remember, it is very important to actually write down what you learn during these homework exercises. You will be using the information gained during these exercises throughout your thinking straight work.

Discriminating is the next **Little D**. Once you have detected the bleeps on your psychological radar screen, it is necessary to determine whether these bleeps are friend or foe. Are the thoughts, feelings, and actions that you've detected helping you to reach your goals? Are they enhancing to self, others, and relationships? Are they based on facts, logical, and flexible? Are they improving your mood, assisting you to think more productively, and helping you behave and act healthfully and appropriately?

If the answers are yes, what you have detected on your radar screen are probably "friends." As you will learn in the next chapter, these actions and thoughts are based on **Rational Beliefs**.

But what if you discover that these bleeps are defeating and destructive to self, others, and relationships? What if they are rigid, blocking your improved mood and productive actions? What if they keep you from solving problems and generally just get in your way?

If this is the case, chances are you have detected **Irrational Beliefs** that lead to an inappropriate emotional and behavioral consequences. You have met the enemy! These unhealthy responses will certainly get in your way in achieving your goals and will most likely block your pursuit of happiness and contentment.

You will use the final **Little D** in order to attack the enemy. The third Little D is **Disputing** (or Debating) those unhealthy and irrational beliefs that largely create the unhealthy and defeating emotional and behavioral consequences. When we're feeling depressed, angry, anxious, and frustrated, it means that it's time to put our unhealthy, irrational beliefs on trial. Disputing refers to the process of forcefully, passionately, and actively challenging the beliefs to see if we can support them with evidence, beyond the shadow of a doubt. As you practice successful disputing, you will become a scientist of sorts, looking for any logical proof or evidence to support the detected beliefs.

20

IT'S NOT AS BAD AS IT SEEMS

Most of us grow up blindly believing certain things, even if these attitudes and assumptions (beliefs) are not in our best interests. It is these personal rules of living[2] that we tell ourselves to obey, such as, "I must be perfect," "People must love me," or "In order to be a good person, I must be successful in all undertakings or else I am a total failure," that are the enemies of happiness and psychological wellness. In Chapter Four, you will learn even more specific skills about the disputing process.

E: Effects

So far, you've learned about the A, B, C, and D of thinking straight. There is also an E, F, and G.

The **E** stands for **Effects**, specifically, the effects of disputing. When we have detected what Alcoholics Anonymous refers to as **"Stinking Thinking,"** and we have debated, challenged, and changed these irrational beliefs, there are rewards, and the rewards are many! We replace the unhealthy pattern of thinking with a set of effective beliefs, assumptions, thoughts, and attitudes that help us create and maintain our own happiness. We also notice that we feel in a more appropriate, effective, and enhancing way. We also act and behave in ways that are self-, other-, and relationship-enhancing. We are able to create a personal philosophy based on wants, wishes, preferences, and desires. This new philosophy is now based on flexibility that can help us to solve problems more effectively, deal with emotional upset, and act in ways that are in our short-term and long-term best interest.

Our magical video equipment now begins to record a whole different pattern of thinking and acting. Though we are still placed in difficult situations and must deal with difficult people, we can handle these much more effectively. We may notice increased self-enhancement, more scientific and flexible thinking, a healthier outlook on our situation, and a new ability to just have fun and enjoy life. This effective philosophy also leads to greater and healthier self-interests and self-direction, increased social interests, higher frustration tolerance, acceptance of uncertainty, and commitment to creative pursuits.[3]

IT'S NOT AS BAD AS IT SEEMS

F: Feelings

The **F** in our new alphabet of thinking straight stands for **Feelings**. After we have successfully detected and disputed our underlying Irrational Beliefs, we have created not only a new set of healthy or rational beliefs, but also a new set of appropriate feelings. Don't be surprised when you have successfully disputed underlying irrational beliefs and still feel bad!

Remember, the goal is not to feel good and "be happy" all the time, but to change unhealthy and defeating beliefs in order to feel and act more appropriately. Change is measured in intensity, duration, and frequency. If something really bad has happened to you, and you begin to feel depressed, successful disputing will result not in feeling good, but in feeling appropriately. You may find yourself still feeling sad and disappointed, but these appropriate negative emotions will help you move forward. After successful disputing when you're feeling angry, you may continue to feel highly irritated, but irritation, unlike intense anger and rage, rarely blocks people from achieving their goals.

I want to repeat and emphasize this idea. The "thinking straight" approach of Rational-Emotive Therapy teaches that **appropriate** negative and positive feelings are significantly and importantly different from **inappropriate** negative and positive feelings. Appropriate feelings like sorrow, regret, irritation, annoyance, disappointment, concern, etc. can be thought to range from light to heavy, or perhaps from 0 to 99. Inappropriate negative feelings like depression, anger, rage, frustration, and anxiety can also vary in intensity and might be thought to start at 101 and go to 200 or even higher! People can have different levels of appropriate negative feelings such as strong disappointment, sorrow, or grief and be quite healthy psychologically, but even slight depression serves to warn us that something unhealthy is probably going on.

In rating feelings, it would be better to have two separate scales: one that measures appropriate negative feelings (from 0 to 99) and one that measures inappropriate negative feelings (ranging from 101 to 200). However, for the sake of simplicity, I like to use an intensity scale that ranges from 0 to 10. The "0" range means that I have not been feeling any particular emotion. The "1 - 4" range usually represents emotions that may be negative but quite appropriate. For example, if you plan to go shopping but you can't because your car has a flat tire, it's likely that you would feel negatively, but perhaps only mildly annoyed and disappointed.

A feeling of "5" on the intensity scale would mean that the emotional reaction is right on the border between healthy and unhealthy.

Once the emotion moves in the "6 - 10" range, I think of the feelings as having crossed into the unhealthy, inappropriate, and defeating range. If your car had a flat tire, you couldn't go shopping, and you reacted with intense anger and kicked a hole in the wall, these feelings and behaviors are anything but healthy.

I want you to start using this 0 - 10 point intensity scale as you monitor your feelings and actions. Think of the emotions in the 0 - 4 range as being based on healthy thinking (rational beliefs), while those in the 6 - 10 range as representing reactions based on unhealthy, defeating thinking (irrational beliefs). If after disputing the "stinking thinking," you still feel in the 6 - 10 range, chances are your disputation has not been completely successful. But don't worry. Think of this as simply being a flashing yellow light that warns you to go back and begin looking for underlying irrational beliefs, and to continue the disputing process in a more forceful way. (A copy of a Daily Mood Record with instructions is included in the Appendix section of this book, and you can copy and use this form.)

G: Goals

Finally, **G** stands for **Goals**. The RET thinking straight approach to happiness emphasizes being able to set and achieve realistic and healthy goals. To do this, you'll need to apply the other letters of the thinking straight alphabet. To successfully set and reach these goals, it is important to continually remind yourself of the "B-C Connection." The **B-C Connection** stands for the relationship between our underlying beliefs and our emotional and behavioral consequences.

As we discussed in Chapter One, many people think that if only they had the right job, more money, or other such "things,"

then they would be happy. They are depending on outside activators to "make" them happy. Let's call this the "A-C Connection"
of unhappiness. The A-C Connection says that people feel and act
in direct relation to outside events (activators).

But the B-C Connection says that we feel and act largely
because of our outlook, thoughts, and attitudes (beliefs). Stop and
consider this for a moment. Your video camera records you thinking, "He made me so angry!" Is that an A-C or a B-C Connection?

It's an A-C Connection statement. The idea is that a person
feels angry because of something the other person did. Remember,
other people may be activators but they are not godlike creators.

As we increasingly accept the B-C Connection, we give
ourselves a great deal of power and control and can reduce our sense
of helplessness and powerlessness. In the next chapter, you will
learn how certain beliefs are related to particular feelings, and how
these beliefs reduce our personal sense of power and control.
You'll also learn more about disputing and challenging underlying
stinking thinking.

Suggested Homework for Chapter Two:

Review the journal that you have been keeping. Using your
special video equipment, identify a situation in which you reacted
with intense and defeating emotions and actions. Write down the
answers to the following questions:

1. What were the specific defeating emotions and actions?
Rate the feelings on the 0 - 10 point intensity scale discussed earlier.

2. What were the defeating actions and behaviors that
occurred? Be very specific in describing these.

IT'S NOT AS BAD AS IT SEEMS

    3. What was the activator that happened just before you felt and acted the way you did? Be specific in describing the activator.

    4. What went through your mind at Point B, concerning the beliefs about the activator? Write down everything that you can remember thinking.

    (Even better, when you are in a situation and find yourself feeling and acting in an intense and defeating way, take a minute to write down the thoughts you are having so you can use this information for homework assignments.)

    When you completed this assignment were you able to actually feel some of those defeating, negative, unhealthy emotions? Can you see how the "B-C Connection" in this situation, and not the actual event, is creating those emotions? The actual event has already happened, so now it is simply the fact that you are remembering and thinking about the situation that creates your feelings. Could you create a different outlook right now that would change your feelings about the activator?

    Some people rely on rationalizing rather than rational thinking and just try to "think positively" about bad situations. While this might help temporarily, the goal of thinking straight is to develop a set of beliefs and philosophies that result in feeling better and getting better, not only for the moment but for years to come.

CHAPTER THREE

When the Shoulds Hit the Fan

Ever since I was a small child, I have detested liver. I have made several attempts to develop a taste for this food, and have even tried eating liver in fancy restaurants. No matter how hard I try, I just can't seem to enjoy, or even tolerate, eating liver.

I also don't particularly like butter brickle ice cream, nor do I enjoy watching "slapstick" comedies. Since I've told you that I don't like liver, butter brickle ice cream, or slapstick comedies, what do we know about these things? Are liver, butter brickle ice cream, or slapstick comedies good? Are they bad?

In Chapter One, we talked a lot about outlook. When it comes to likes and dislikes, we are very often talking about outlook, taste, and **Preference**. Realistically speaking, liver is liver! As Shakespeare said in *Hamlet*, it is neither good nor bad (even though it may be good for us). We like or dislike certain foods, movies or TV shows based largely on our preferences and personal outlooks.

It's that "B-C Connection" that we talked about in Chapter Two that largely determines our reactions to certain activators, events, or situations. I am pretty well convinced that my dislike for liver is not genetic since both of my parents love liver. (By the way, I also don't think my dislike for liver was based on any early trauma, since my parents never forced me to eat liver!)

It is really no big deal when people dislike certain foods, TV shows, or movies. However, in some situations, when our outlook changes and begins to become rather crooked and disturbed, more serious consequences can occur. When this happens, we may begin to block our happiness. People can often begin to have difficulty in their pursuit of happiness, but also begin to experience problems such as depression, anxiety, panic, frustration, and anger. In this chapter, you will learn about the specific types of "stinking thinking" that create emotional upset and prevent us from developing contentment and enjoying life.

In Rational-Emotive Therapy (RET), Dr. Ellis emphasizes that at the root of almost all unhappiness there is a set of shoulds, musts, oughts, have-tos, and got-tos.[1] When these "shoulds hit the fan," they often result in considerable unhappiness, disturbance, and an overall lack of contentment. These are absolutistic, dogmatic shoulds which take the form of internal commandments and demands.

Remember, these are irrational shoulds, and not shoulds of preference (for example, "You should preferably treat children kindly"), empirical shoulds ("You should get water if you mix two parts of hydrogen and one part of oxygen"), or shoulds of recommendation ("You should really go see that new movie at the theater").[2] In this chapter, you will learn to recognize the "shoulds" and other forms of "stinking," irrational thinking that largely create our unhappiness.

Musturbation

Dr. Ellis has coined a word that I want you to commit to memory - **Musturbation.** Musturbation[3] refers to both the general and specific "shoulds" that result in upset and unhappiness. These aren't "preferential shoulds" as in, "You really should see that movie," but rather, they are a basic pattern of irrational thinking.

Musturbation is the absolutistic thinking that takes place when human beings begin to "play God" and demand or insist that they be different, others be different, or the world be different.

Three Types of Shoulds

The first type of musturbation occurs when we develop commandments, demands, shoulds, and musts about ourselves. For example, it is not unusual for us to think, "In order to be an okay person, I must do well in my job." Another form of "shoulding on" ourselves is to maintain the outlook, "I must be loved by important people in my life, and if not, I'm unlovable and it's awful." We also often develop the outlook that we must succeed and reach all goals or else we are somehow less of a person. These demands that are placed on ourselves often lead to depression, shame, guilt, and anxiety.

The second specific type of "should" that hits the fan is in the form of demands that we place on others. We may believe that if we treat others kindly, they must and should treat us with equal fairness and kindness. This represents what has been called the "reverse Golden Rule" in which we demand, "Do unto me as I do unto thee!" We may also believe that if people don't treat us the way that they absolutely *must*, they are damnable human beings who should be punished for their wrongdoing. When we maintain the belief that other human beings must treat us in a particular way, there are often problems with anger and rage. It is a safe bet that if we are feeling intense anger toward another person, then we are probably internally or externally demanding that somehow they be different than they are.

The third basic type of should is based on demands that we create about how the world, and life in general, should be. Here, people often believe that life *should* be fair, and if it is not, it is terrible, awful, and that the unfairness just can't be tolerated. If we maintain the belief that the world must be fair, or otherwise we can't stand it, such a belief often leads to problems with frustration, anger, and self-pity. Along with this underlying irrational belief, there are often problems with procrastination as well as addictive behaviors such as abuse of alcohol or other drugs. For example, people may maintain the belief that life conditions should be such that they feel good all the time, otherwise they must create synthetic good feelings by using alcohol or drugs.

So, it's these three types of "shoulds that hit the fan" that often keep people from finding happiness and create various forms of emotional upset.

Challenging the Shoulds

I hope that right now you are questioning some of the ideas that are being presented. Perhaps you're thinking, "But if I treat people kindly, they really *should* treat me with equal kindness!" Or maybe you're thinking, "But if I work hard on my job, my boss really *must* appreciate and reward me or my hard work!" You may even be thinking, "But I really *do* need love and approval in order to be happy!"

In the next chapter, we will look specifically at ways to get "the shoulds off the fan," but right now, let's begin to challenge some of these basic shoulds.

Within the universe, there are some fundamental absolutes and laws of physics and other physical laws. An example is the law of gravity, which governs what will happen to certain objects if dropped in earth's atmosphere. Right now, stand up, get a coin, and drop the coin. What happened? Unless you're reading this book in outer space, the coin dropped. The coin fell because of the law of gravity, which commands that in our atmosphere, objects *must* fall to the earth.

However, where is the law of the universe that says that when we treat people fairly, they *must* treat us with equal kindness? True, there may be moral or Scriptural guidelines that encourage us to do unto others as we would want them to do unto us. But if this was an absolute law of the universe, then what would happen when we treated people kindly and fairly? People would indeed "automatically" treat us fairly, and life conditions would "automatically" be fair.

Regrettably, there are no such universal laws! But as humans, we often want to magically pretend that such laws exist, and when we try to do so, using the three basic musts, we almost always end up feeling bad and having subsequent behavioral and emotional problems.

Musturbation, then, is the most basic form of "stinking thinking," and as such, it is the most popular form of irrational thinking. As we discussed in Chapter Two, these shoulds are irrational because they cannot be supported, are inflexible, block our attempts to gain happiness and contentment, and are defeating and destructive to self, others, and relationships.

IT'S NOT AS BAD AS IT SEEMS

From musturbation, there come four derivatives: awfulizing, "I-can't-stand-it-itis," damnation, and specific thinking errors such as always-and-never thinking.[4] That is, when people tend to maintain the irrational beliefs based on the three basic musts or shoulds, they then tend to draw irrational conclusions. These irrational conclusions also play a big part in creating unhappiness and inefficiency.

Awfulizing

One type of irrational conclusion that people create is called "**Awfulizing.**" Dr. Ellis originated the word "**catastrophizing**" to show us that people tend to take little inconveniences or dangers and turn them into catastrophes. However, we don't stop there! When bad things happen, or dangers or inconveniences take place, we also tend to **awfulize, terribleize,** or **horribleize**, says Dr. Ellis.

When people awfulize, terribleize, or horribleize, they draw the conclusion and maintain the belief that some situation is 100 percent bad or even more than 100 percent bad. While bad things do happen to us all the time (although some people do seem to get more than their fair share!), to maintain the belief that these things are "awful" would mean that the outcome would not be just bad, but 100 percent bad, if not 101 percent bad.

Stop and think for a second. What is there in this world that is in fact 100 percent bad? I personally believe that some things may approach 100 percent, but can anything equal or exceed 100 percent bad? Somebody once challenged me on this and asked, "Well, tell me, Ed, what if you were captured and subjected to a slow, torturous death? Wouldn't that be awful?" I thought for a minute and responded, "I agree that such torture would be very, very bad. But isn't it true that there could always be a form of torture that could be even more painful, even slower?"

In the early 1980s, I had an opportunity to examine my own tendency to awfulize. In 1982, for some unknown reason, I fainted in a store and my head struck the corner of a counter. This resulted in a near-fatal injury. In fact, the attending physicians notified my parents and stated that it would be advisable for them to travel to Memphis, since in all likelihood, I would die. I awakened in intensive care, with numerous tubes coming out of my head, and various machines attached to my body. I had no hair as a result of brain surgery, and only half a beard.

After the initial thoughts of gratitude for being alive, one of the first thoughts that came to my mind was, "How bad is this?" My assessment was that this injury and the subsequent surgery and inconvenience was probably 30 percent bad, at the very worst. However, I could also have considered it 100 percent bad, and could have thought to myself, "This is awful! I'll be out of work for some time, which will result in a reduction in my income! People may look at my hairless head and laugh! What if there is damage done, and my memory is not as good?" All of these thoughts would have been a form of awfulizing and catastrophizing which probably would have resulted in some form of anxiety, panic, tension, and nervousness.

One warning sign of awfulizing is the use of "what if?" thinking. "What if he or she doesn't like me?" "What if I don't get the job I really want?" Usually, when I hear these statements, I begin to wonder if there is not some additional thinking going on, which is, " . . . and if that happens, it will be absolutely **AWFUL!**"

Don't forget to use your special video recording machine in order to start detecting those times when you rely on "what if" thinking with accompanying awfulizing. If you find yourself feeling intensely anxious or nervous (beyond appropriate concern), begin immediately to look for your own catastrophizing and awfulizing.

I-Can't-Stand-It-Itis

A second irrational conclusion that people often develop is based on a form of thinking referred to in Rational-Emotive Therapy as "**I-Can't-Stand-It-Itis.**" This almost always results in intense frustration and is a symptom that people suffer from who have **Low Frustration Tolerance** (LFT).

IT'S NOT AS BAD AS IT SEEMS

I-Can't-Stand-It-Itis is my own favorite. It is the underlying irrational belief that I maintain in many situations, and the type of "stinking thinking" that I continue to forcefully work on changing.

Think for a minute about what "I can't stand it" really means. If you had a job that you really liked, and unexpectedly you were fired, what would happen? There might be a number of changes that would occur, but if you believed that you really couldn't stand losing your job, you would most likely feel intense frustration. If you literally could not stand something, what would happen? You would drop dead on the spot! But listen to how many times each day you think or say, "I can't stand it!" How many times each day do you die a natural death?

Since there have been no reported cases of natural deaths based on I-Can't-Stand-It-Itis, the evidence is overwhelming that, in fact, we *can* stand *practically* anything. If I were captured by terrorists and tortured, I could stand the torture until these acts resulted in my death. If I were in an airplane at 35,000 feet that suddenly lost power and began falling to the earth, I could stand the discomfort for the time required until the airplane struck the earth. At that point, I would most likely not survive, though not because of the belief that "I can't stand it" but rather because of the injuries sustained in the crash.

We do ourselves a huge disservice when we nurture our low frustration tolerance and hold onto the belief that we "can't stand" certain people, places, or things. LFT is often associated with over-eating, abusing alcohol and other drugs, procrastinating, and developing other emotional and behavioral problems.

I-Can't-Stand-It-Itis is often found in individuals who believe that "They want what they want when they want it, and they should get it without delay, pain, or effort." This belief centers on the self-statement and belief that we cannot bear discomfort and unpleasantness, and therefore we must get what we want. I've known people who have said that they "couldn't stand" people who spread gossip about them. Have you ever known anyone who died of natural causes just because someone gossiped about them?

How much do you suffer from low frustration tolerance? How often do you say or think that you can't stand something? As you are rating your various emotional reactions, chances are if you feel frustration above a "5," there exists a strong degree of I-Can't-Stand-It-Itis.

Damnation

The third derivative from musturbation is "**Damnation.**" This type of irrational thinking involves our tendency to be excessively critical, damning of ourselves, others, and/or life conditions.

Self-rating and **self-downing** is, in my opinion, a particularly wicked form of irrational thinking. Humans seem to be biologically predisposed to play this "rating game," and the rules of this game are simple: I do something, and almost immediately I globally rate myself and damn myself. I rate not what I did, but rather my entire being. I conclude that because I perhaps failed at something or did something incorrectly, I am therefore a total, 100 percent failure as a person. We unmercifully put ourselves down. For example, "My marriage failed, therefore, I am a total, worthless failure."

In the Bible, there are teachings that emphasize, "Condemn the sin, but not the sinner." Rather than evaluating our actions, characteristics, and behaviors, in self-damnation we are prone to condemn and down our entire personhood. When we engage in self-damnation, we end up almost always feeling depressed and guilty.

Under what conditions could we be total failures as human beings? A horse is what percentage a horse? Fifty percent? Ninety-two percent? A horse is, of course, 100 percent a horse. If not, we would have a mule, or a donkey, or some other hybrid animal.

Likewise, if I am in fact a failure as a human being, then by definition I must be 100 percent a failure. This would mean that I have in the past, am in the present, and will in the future, fail at *every* aspect of my life. I would fail at tying my shoes, at brushing my teeth, at walking, talking or listening. I would fail all the time!

IT'S NOT AS BAD AS IT SEEMS

Because we are what Dr. Ellis refers to as **"FMHB's,"** that is, **"Fallible, Messed-up Human Beings,"** with the incurable tendency to make mistakes, we will certainly and consistently fail at certain things. Despite five years of private piano lessons, I failed to become a good pianist. Despite some degree of hard work, I failed Advanced Calculus when I was in college. However, because of these failures, did it mean that I had suddenly become a "total failure?" *Au contraire!* I was then, and I continue to be today, a human, with relative strengths and weaknesses, who will indeed fail at certain things. However, because I'm made up of millions of characteristics, traits, and behaviors, there is little likelihood that I will be a total failure in all of these areas.

When you think of yourself (or another) as being a total failure, ask yourself if there is anything that you do successfully.

There are people in history who are remembered for their despicable behavior and the intensely negative impact they had on history and humankind. Is it possible that despite their intensely bad behavior, there was anything about them that could be considered a good characteristic? Were they perhaps protective of family members? Kind to animals? Generous to charitable organizations?

It is extremely hard work to separate the actions from the person. But when we feel depressed, chances are we are equating our own characteristics, traits, and actions with our total value as human beings.

I encourage you to evaluate behavior and actions, because when you do, you may discover that some of your characteristics or behaviors aren't so terrific. But only with this initial information can you work diligently to change and improve in these areas. However, when you are busy playing God and condemning yourself, it becomes almost impossible to change because you are feeling so inadequate, guilty, and depressed.

Dr. Richard Wessler once used a drawing (on the next page) to illustrate the idea of rating the person rather than rating the behavior.[5] The drawing is a portrait of you, me, our friends, enemies, politicians, and, in fact, every human in the universe. We are made up of millions of traits, characteristics, and behaviors which are the small dots in the circle. We also have roles such as parent, child, friend, employee, spouse, to name just a few.

Some of our characteristic "dots" are terrific. For example, we freely volunteer our time to help others, we listen attentively to

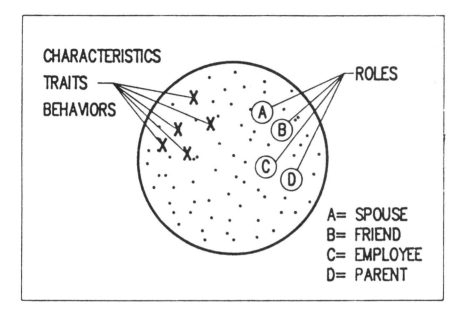

Characteristics, Acts, And Behaviors
Do Not Equal Personhood

our spouses, we work hard, and so on. But, because we are all FMHBs some of the "dots" aren't so great. Maybe there is the tendency to overeat, act impatiently, curs too much, or act irritably. I've put "Xs" over these not-so-great characteristics. Sometimes roles change, and we are no longer a spouse or an employee, for example. There's an "X" over these roles as well.

So, what's left after I've eliminated some of the not-so-good characteristics, traits, and behaviors, and after some of our roles or jobs are eliminated? Does the person stop existing? Does having some bad parts make the whole person totally disappear?

No! The person is still there, and still has probably millions of other traits, behaviors, and characteristics that are positively fantastic. Even when some roles such as "spouse" aren't there anymore, it doesn't mean that all jobs and roles are eliminated. Use this drawing to remind yourself that even while you may **HAVE** weaknesses and failures, you are not a **FAILURE** as a person.

Damnation is not limited to simply rating and downing ourselves. We may also have a tendency to globally rate and down other people. We may conclude that our bosses, our mates, our children, or our parents are totally rotten. We conclude that they are 100 per cent bad.

Other-downing results in intense feelings of anger. This anger, again, makes it difficult to solve problems, get along with other people, and communicate effectively with the people with whom we do feel intensely angry. But when we begin to objectively and critically evaluate the tendency to damn others, we learn that, just like us, they are not totally bad.

We may also be prone to damn our life conditions. We may rate our lives as being totally worthless, or the conditions under which we live as being totally damnable and unbearable. This can result in our feeling powerless, hopeless, and helpless. If we view our life conditions as being totally bad, then there is little motivation to work at enjoying life. Life conditions can at times be bad, but are they totally damnable?

Thinking Errors

We have discussed some of the "shoulds that hit the fan," including musturbation and its derivatives, awfulizing, I-Can't - Stand-It-Itis, and Damnation (of self and others, and/or life).

In addition to these, there are also some specific types of **Cognitive Distortions**, or "**Thinking Errors**," that intefere with our ability to find happiness and maintain psychological well-being. These have been described by Dr. Aaron Beck[6] and Dr. David Burns[7,8] in what is known as **Cognitive Therapy,** which was developed by Dr. Beck. Rational-Emotive Therapy and Cognitive Therapy are similar, since both emphasize the relationship between how we think and how we feel.

Dr. Burns, in his book, *Feeling Good: The New Mood Therapy* and in his more recent book, *The Feeling Good Handbook*, specifically describes these types of cognitive distortions as "thinking errors."

The first type of thinking error is referred to as "**All-or-Nothing Thinking**." People with this type of distortion see things in a black-and-white fashion, and often demand of themselves that they perform perfectly, with anything less than that being viewed as total failure. When you indulge in all-or-nothing thinking, it is quite easy to make yourself depressed when you eventually fall short of your goals.

The second such error is called "**Overgeneralization**." You may make a mistake in one situation and quickly conclude that this single episode proves that you will continue in a never-ending pattern of similar defeat.

The "**Mental Filter**" is a thinking error in which a person picks out one single negative detail and dwells on it exclusively. When this happens, our vision of reality becomes colored by the filter, often resulting in feelings of depression.

Another type of cognitive distortion or thinking error is "**Disqualifying the Positive**." Here, we are prone to disregard or reject positive experiences by insisting that "they don't count."

"**Jumping to Conclusions**" is another common type of thinking error in which we form negative interpretations or impressions about certain people or things even though we lack facts or support for our conclusions. Two specific types of jumping to conclusions errors include "**Mind Reading**" and "**Fortune Telling**." In mind reading, we conclude that someone is reacting negatively to us, but we don't bother to check this out. For example, we might believe that because someone frowns when they look at us, it means that they don't like us. In fortune telling, we anticipate that things will turn out badly. We are convinced that our prediction is established fact, and tend to behave in a fashion consistent with our prediction.

IT'S NOT AS BAD AS IT SEEMS

"**Magnification**" or "**Minimization**" are other types of thinking errors. We tend to magnify the importance of negative events, such as mistakes that we have made, while minimizing the importance of successful actions or accomplishments.

"**Emotional Reasoning**" is a thinking error in which we conclude that because we feel a certain way at a certain time, this proves something global about us. For example, if we feel depressed, we may conclude that we are depressed and will always be depressed.

"**Labeling**" and "**Mislabeling**" are other types of thinking errors. Labeling is an extreme form of overgeneralization in which we label ourselves in a negative fashion rather than labeling the error or behavior as such. For example, if we make a mistake and conclude, "I'm a total failure," we are erroneously labeling ourselves rather than the action. Mislabeling occurs when we describe an event with highly colored and emotionally charged language which only serves to increase our emotional upset.

"**Personalization**" is another type of thinking error. In it we exclusively blame ourselves for some negative external event over which we may have had little or no control. I knew somebody who once made a mistake at work and held himself totally responsible for this error and personalized the blame. In fact, there were three or four levels of review and within each the mistake could have been detected. Rather than share the responsibility with co-workers, he berated himself and personalized the responsibility.

So, when the shoulds (and their derivatives such as awfulizing, damnation, I-Can't-Stand-It-Itis and specific thinking errors) hit the fan, problems arise. These specific forms of irrational beliefs and thinking errors block our happiness and make things seem much worse than they actually are.

We know that the shoulds are hitting the fan when we begin to feel extremely upset such as being depressed (not just disappointed or sad), intensely angry (not just annoyed), highly frustrated (not just mildly irritated) and anxious (not just mildly concerned). Further, we have clues that our shoulds are hitting the fan when we start to act in ways that are destructive and defeating to ourselves, to others, and to relationships.

IT'S NOT AS BAD AS IT SEEMS

Cold, Warm and Hot Thoughts

As you learn to identify your personal forms of irrational thinking, begin to picture a thinking thermometer that measures the temperature of our thoughts. Rational-Emotive Therapy distinguishes between **cold, warm** and **hot thoughts.**[9] The thermometer might look something like this (below).

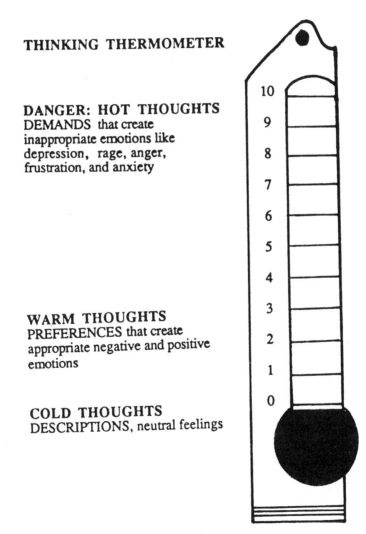

THINKING THERMOMETER

DANGER: HOT THOUGHTS
DEMANDS that create
inappropriate emotions like
depression, rage, anger,
frustration, and anxiety

WARM THOUGHTS
PREFERENCES that create
appropriate negative and positive
emotions

COLD THOUGHTS
DESCRIPTIONS, neutral feelings

10
9
8
7
6
5
4
3
2
1
0

Cold cognitions, or **cold thoughts,** are simply objective observations or descriptions. For example, as I sit in my office, I see a brown sofa. The statement, "There is a brown sofa," is simply a description and would be a "cold" thought or cold cognition. The person who made the mistake at work might also simply make the statement, "I made a mistake at work." Such thoughts generally result in no emotional reaction.

Warm cognitions and **warm thoughts** are evaluations that emphasize preferences and nonpreferences rather than commands or absolutes. For example, I might think, "I have a brown sofa in my office and I really wish I had selected a different color. I didn't so that's too bad." There still remains a description. With it, there still is a preference expressed.

The person who made the mistake at work might first think descriptively, "I made a mistake," and then add the warm thought, "And I really wish I hadn't made the mistake. However, the reality of the situation is that I did make a mistake, and while it's too bad, it's not the end of the world."

During such warm cognitions or warm thoughts, we do experience emotional reactions. However, as we have discussed in Chapter Two, these emotional reactions are appropriate and healthy. I might feel disappointed and perhaps even annoyed that I didn't select another color of sofa for my office, and the person who made the mistake at work might feel quite disappointed and sad about the mistake. With such appropriate negative emotional reactions, the strong likelihood exists that we will be able to cope effectively with the situation.

When having cold and warm cognitions, people rarely if ever experience emotional upset or psychological difficulties. However, when our thinking thermometer creeps into the hot range, problems erupt. **Hot Thoughts,** like warm thoughts, are evaluations, but rather than emphasizing wants, wishes, and preferences, these hot thoughts emphasize absolutes and commands, and are based on the rigid shoulds discussed in this chapter.

Back to my sofa, I might think, "I have a brown sofa (cold thought), I wish I had bought a different color (warm thought), and therefore I should have known better! How stupid of me to not have realized my mistake earlier!" (hot thoughts). The person who made a mistake at work may well have thought, "I made a mistake (cold thought), I wish I hadn't made the mistake (warm thought), I should not have made the mistake (hot thought), and am clearly a total failure because I did!" (hot thought).

Use your thinking thermometer as you continue to work your thinking straight approach to happiness. Remember that *cold thoughts* usually have no particular emotions associated with them, and we generally feel "neutral."

Warm thoughts lead to mild emotions such as concern, regret, sorrow, mild frustration and annoyance, as well as pleasure, and satisfaction. These warm thoughts are based on wants, wishes, and preferences, and lead to self-, other-, and relationship-enhancing outcomes. Warm thoughts are actually **Rational Beliefs**, which help us to achieve our goals and maximize our happiness.

Hot thoughts usually lead to emotional upset and disturbance with severe feelings of anxiety, panic, depression, intense anger, rage, inadequacy, and positive exaggerations about ourselves (grandiosity). Hot thoughts are the **Irrational Beliefs** that are self-, other-, and relationship-defeating. This pattern of hot thinking results in not only emotional problems but also behavioral problems such as angry outbursts and procrastination.

The Rational-Emotive Therapy thinking straight approach can help you to identify your underlying shoulds that keep hitting the fan. You now have a better understanding of the specific types of underlying irrational beliefs (hot thoughts), and the kinds of emotional upset and problems associated with the various types of irrational beliefs such as musturbation, awfulizing, I-Can't-Stand-It-Itis, and damnation. Additionally, you have read about certain types of thinking errors such as all-or-nothing thinking, overgeneralization, jumping to conclusions, and others, all of which play a role in interfering with our pursuit of happiness.

In Chapter One, you started keeping a diary in which you identified feelings of anger and frustration and rated these emotions on a 0- to 10-point scale. In Chapter Two, you were more specific in identifying both the activators which happened just before you felt and acted in a self-, other-, or relationship-defeating way as well as the resulting emotional consequences. You also began to more specifically monitor the particular types of beliefs and attitudes that lead to these feelings and actions. And now it's time to apply what you've learned in Chapter Three.

Suggested Homework for Chapter Three:

(1)   Review your diary and identify some of the specific situations in which you felt emotional upset. Now recreate one situation in your head and pick out the specific types of irrational beliefs associated with this emotion. (For example, the person who made the mistake at work might have felt depressed. In all likelihood, this depression was created not by the mistake, but rather by the self-downing and self-damnation. He may have thought of himself as a total failure and a worthless human being because of this mistake. Such thoughts lead to depressed feelings.) In your situation, what were some of the underlying beliefs and selfstatements?

If you felt extremely anxious, look for awfulizing, catastrophizing, and terribleizing. If you felt angry, look for the shoulds, musts, commands, and other forms of absolutistic thinking such as "playing God" and demanding that whatever was wrong somehow magically be different. Finally, if you felt highly frustrated, look for LFT (low frustration tolerance) and the dread disease of I-Can't-Stand-It-Itis.

Sometimes, finding the underlying irrational beliefs is easier said than done. At times, we may notice some negative thoughts

42

going through our heads, but these may not seem related to the underlying irrational beliefs. These may simply be inferences or what Drs. Beck and Burns call "**Automatic Thoughts.**"

Think of the ocean. There are waves on the surface, beneath the waves there are currents, and even further down, there may be a huge giant shark swimming along which in turn creates some of the currents, which in turn create some of the waves. Think of the currents as being the inferences or automatic thoughts, such as "I can't do anything right," "Nobody likes me," or "Things never go my way." Perhaps you're picking up some of these types of thoughts in your daily examples. The drawing below has been used to illustrate the idea of inferences and deeper underlying core beliefs.

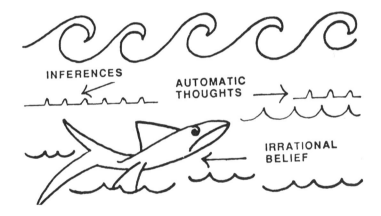

But let's go deeper. Using a strategy called the "**Vertical Arrow Technique,**"[10] start with the first thought you identified. For example, perhaps you picked up on the thought, "Nobody likes me." Ask yourself, "What if this was indeed true?" That is, what if in reality, nobody liked you? What thought comes next? For example, you might then think, "I'll never have any friends." Then ask yourself, "And what if this was in fact true, and I would never have any friends? What would this say about me?" Perhaps then you might answer, "There is really something wrong with me." Next, continue going deeper by asking yourself, "And what would it say about me if there was something wrong with me?"

IT'S NOT AS BAD AS IT SEEMS

Chances are, as you dive deeper, you will uncover your own personal, destructive **shark** swimming way beneath the surface. Perhaps this shark is self-damnation, which represents the core, hot, irrational belief, "I am a failure, I'm worthless, and I'm unlovable." I want you to become a shark hunter (complete with shark repellant) in order to identify your own underlying "sharks" of irrational thinking. (**S-H-A-R-K** has special meaning. It will not only represent your irrational beliefs but it's also an abbreviation or shorthand technique that you will learn to use later.)

Perhaps in another situation you find yourself feeling intensely angry. What are the first inferences or automatic thoughts that you pick up on?

Use the downward arrow technique and keep asking yourself, "And what would this mean?" Also ask yourself, "And what would this say about me, the situation, or the other person?" As you use the downward arrow technique, most likely you will eventually hunt down the shark and uncover the underlying should or form of musturbation that is responsible for your feeling angry.

Before you start reading Chapter Four, identify at least four situations in which you have found yourself feeling intensely upset. Identify the sharks, the underlying irrational beliefs. In Chapter Four, you will learn how to challenge these beliefs and replace them with more rational, warm, and healthy ways of thinking.

CHAPTER FOUR

Just the Facts, Folks:
How to Get the Shoulds Off the Fan

Do you believe in Santa Claus? How about the Easter Bunny? Do you believe that a living, ten-foot monster is in your attic?

When I was a young child, I believed in Santa Claus, the Easter Bunny, and sometimes, monsters. And most people that I know say that they did, too, when they were young. So how come we no longer believe in Santa Claus, the Easter Bunny, or other such characters?

As for me, my parents provided me with certain information and facts, and with this, I began to gradually change my thinking about the existence of a living, breathing Santa Claus.

Challenging Irrational Beliefs

It is interesting that in certain cases, we quite passionately and vigorously challenge the factual basis of some of our dearly held beliefs and ideas. But when it comes to our underlying irrational beliefs that only serve to create unhappiness, we are much less likely to challenge these notions.

Many of our irrational beliefs are formed early in life. For whatever reason, we may view ourselves as being inadequate and incapable and may go through life accepting this belief as 100 percent factually correct. We will challenge the existence of Santa Claus, or the Easter Bunny, but we accept blindly the beliefs that result in considerable unhappiness, upset, and ineffectiveness. It is almost as if we think, "Well, my crazy mother, father, teacher, brother, sister, grandmother (or whoever), said so, therefore it *must* be true!"

Once the beliefs are firmly in place and the irrational belief shark is swimming around, we easily find support for our nutty beliefs. For example, if a person deeply believes that he or she is a failure, the smallest mistake becomes proof positive for the core belief. The person who has panic or anxiety attacks, and experiences the slightest physical sensation, sees this as being evidence that another panic attack is about to occur, which triggers even more awfulizing and catastrophizing.

In the old television show, "Dragnet," Sgt. Friday would frequently state, "Just the facts, ma'am." This chapter is based on the notion that much of what we tell ourselves and believe is not based on "just the facts." While we may be convinced that what we believe represents objective truth, in all likelihood, those beliefs that create an emotional upset are based on "magical thinking" and irrational beliefs, and anything but the facts.

In this chapter, I want you to begin to challenge many of your beliefs about yourself, others, and the world, and like Sgt. Friday, look for just the facts. I want you to become a scientist and test your beliefs to see if they are, in fact, objective, factual, and based on realistic truth.

As I have said before, this process may sound simple, but it's not. If you have believed in Santa Claus for many, many years, it may be difficult to challenge and change this belief. If English is your native language, it would take persistent hard work to learn a second language, and under stress you might go back to speaking your native language.

Likewise, even after you have successfully identified and challenged irrational beliefs, and have successfully changed them to rational beliefs, you will not suddenly become perfect. Unfortunately, I don't believe we ever kill our underlying sharks, but rather, we learn how to put them back in their cages so that they are harmless. But sometimes the salt water corrodes the cages, the sharks of irrational thinking get out, and we find ourselves thinking crookedly. The skills you learn in this chapter will enable you to quickly dispute the irrational beliefs in order to get those sharks back in their cages.

I want you to imagine that you and I meet for the first time. We're meeting in my office, and in this office, there is a brown sofa, several chairs, and a small butler's table. Imagine in our first meeting that I point to the small table and say, "Please be careful not to harm my dog, and certainly don't put your feet on my dog." You probably would look at me quite perplexed and wonder about my own rational thinking and contact with reality. But you see, I have this deeply ingrained belief that brown four-legged objects are always dogs.

If you apply some of the steps that you've learned earlier in order to differentiate a rational from an irrational belief, it would become clear that the belief that my table is a dog is certainly irrational. Further, if I hold onto this belief and tell people about it, the consequences could be quite negative. People might be somewhat hesitant to work in therapy with a clinical psychologist who believes that tables are dogs!

Prove It!

How might you go about challenging the belief that tables are dogs? This chapter focuses on the **Disputing** which is used to challenge and change irrational beliefs and to get the sharks back in their cages.

When a person is convicted for committing a crime, the evidence must stand up beyond a shadow of a doubt. As you begin disputing your core irrational beliefs, I want you to imagine a psychological court of law, and remember that in order to be true, each belief must be supported beyond a shadow of a doubt. This will require you to passionately and forcefully challenge the belief and look for support.

The main goal of disputing is to prove that underlying irrational beliefs are unproductive, lead to self-defeating emotions, are illogical, and are inconsistent with reality.[1]

47

IT'S NOT AS BAD AS IT SEEMS

For any belief, the fundamental goal is to **PROVE IT!** If I want to believe that my office table is a dog, that's fine, so long as I can prove it beyond a shadow of a doubt. So, the first step in putting the belief on trial is to ask for evidence.

What evidence could I muster that could prove beyond a shadow of a doubt that my brown table is a dog? Well, I might say that it's got four legs, dogs have four legs, therefore, it must be a dog. The next disputation question would then be, "But does having four legs prove beyond a shadow of a doubt that this object is a dog?" To this, I might respond, "Well, it not only has four legs, but it's also brown, and there are brown four-legged dogs!" Again, the disputation question is, "But does the fact that it is brown and has four legs prove beyond a shadow of a doubt that this object is a dog? Are there any other requirements necessary in order to make this object a dog? For example, in order to be a dog, would it need to belong to the animal family?"

Is It Logical?

There are a variety of disputing strategies and techniques that can be used when we put our beliefs on trial. First, you can ask yourself if your belief is fundamentally **Logical**. Irrational beliefs are illogical, whereas rational beliefs are logical.

For example, as you work with me on my underlying belief, you might ask, "Where is the logic that would support that this object is in fact a dog?" Or, you might ask, "Is it logical to believe that just because it has four legs and is brown, this clearly proves that it is a dog?" With these types of disputation questions, we emphasize that the belief is magical in nature rather than being based on logic.

Is It Based on Fact?

Another way to dispute our underlying irrational beliefs is to focus on **Empiricism**. Empiricism means that our belief is capable of being verified, or proved or disproved, by factual observation or experimentation. In other words, the belief is based on realistic **Fact**.

When we use empirical forms of debating, we are able to show that our irrational beliefs are inconsistent with reality. You might simply ask, "Where is the evidence?" As we were doing earlier, you might challenge my belief that my table is a dog by asking repeatedly, "Where is the evidence?"

Is It Going to Benefit You?

Another type of disputation is called **Pragmatic** or **Practical Disputation**. Here, you simply look at the practical consequences of maintaining a particular irrational belief. For example, you might ask me, "How is believing that this table is a dog going to benefit you?" You might also ask, "What are the consequences of maintaining this belief that your table is a dog?"

This form of disputation allows us to see that in most cases, our irrational beliefs have no positive consequences, but usually result in depression, anxiety, or other negative practical results.

My Wife Must Fix Dinner . . .

Let me use another example of challenging our underlying irrational beliefs in order to "get the shoulds off the fan." I once had a client who indicated that he had serious problems dealing with his anger. We uncovered one core irrational belief, which was, "My wife *must* fix dinner for me!" When he arrived home and dinner was on the table, everything was fine. However, on those occasions when he came home and dinner was not ready, he would react with intense anger, shouting and even threatening to harm his wife. Needless to say, such behavior on the part of this individual did not contribute to a warm and loving marital relationship.

I taught this client the various types of disputations that can be used to put irrational beliefs on trial. For example, using the logical disputation, I asked, "I understand that you *want* your wife to have dinner ready when you get home, but just because you *want* it, why *must* she have dinner ready?" I also logically pointed out to this client that just because he wanted something didn't make it so.

IT'S NOT AS BAD AS IT SEEMS

In other words, the emphasis in logical disputation is that it doesn't logically make sense to think that just because we believe something "must" be a certain way, it in fact will be that way.

Using empirical types of disputes, the client was asked, when he arrived home on the night in question, whether or not dinner was on the table. The client looked somewhat puzzled, and indicated that of course it wasn't on the table, and that was what had made him so angry. Factually, just because a person maintains the belief that a situation must be a particular way doesn't mean that in fact it will be. He was then asked where the evidence was for his belief that just because he thought dinner should be ready when he got home, in fact it would somehow magically be that way.

As you use empirical types of disputation, remember that if in fact something had to be, should be, or must be a particular way, and if this represented a universal law of physics, then it would be that way.

If a universal law governed the behavior of people, including the law that wives or husbands must have dinner on the table when husbands or wives arrive home, and if this law was of the same power as the law of gravity, then dinner time would operate according to those laws and dinner would absolutely be on the table every single time the spouse came home at night.

While there are laws governing physics, there are no universal laws and truths that govern our behavior and the behavior of others. Insisting, demanding, and commanding that things be a certain way or that people act in a particular way almost always results in our feeling angry.

So, I pointed out to my client that his wife in fact on that evening had not prepared dinner, and that was reality, not his demands. I asked my client, "You tell me. Did she prepare dinner?" When the answer was no, this again emphasized that because we demand something doesn't mean that it must be that way.

Practical disputations were also used with this client. He was asked what the consequences were when he would become angry, and he described increased marital conflict. So it was pointed out to him that practically, when he held onto his irrational

50

belief and got angry, it interfered with both the relationship and also his potential to get some of the things that he wanted within the relationship.

He was asked, "How does getting angry and upset help? When you think the way that you do (that dinner must be ready when you get home), how does it help with problem solving?" Gradually, the client began to better understand that his beliefs did not help in any way, but rather resulted in negative outcome.

My Table Is a Dog . . .

If you were disputing my belief that the table is really a dog, chances are that you would use all forms of disputation, including empirical, logical, and pragmatic. If you continued to forcefully challenge me to come up with evidence that the table is a dog, I would have a hard time proving my belief beyond a shadow of a doubt.

Further, I would soon recognize that the belief is quite illogical, that just because I think a table is a dog doesn't make it a dog. Practically, I would also realize that as long as I hold onto the belief that my table is a dog, there will be negative consequences, such as fewer clients, problems getting along with people, and other such difficulties.

As I successfully dispute my underlying irrational beliefs and get the sharks back in their cages, I open the door for more rational, self-enhancing beliefs and attitudes. I come to accept that while I might *want* the table to be a dog, it is, in fact, a table.

My client would also realize that while he might strongly prefer that his wife fix dinner, his preference does not somehow become an absolute truth that governs the behavior of other people. He might learn to express his strong preferences, but when his preferences are not met, he might now be better able to accept reality and feel perhaps annoyed or irritated rather than intensely angry.

To review briefly, there are certain questions and statements that can be used during the disputation process. Remember to ask yourself the following questions:

Where is the evidence for my belief?

Is there a universal law that supports my belief?

Where is it written, other than in my head, that what I believe must be true?

Where is the logic for my belief?

What are the benefits from holding onto this irrational belief?

Does this belief help me to accomplish my goals and achieve greater happiness?

Does this belief help to improve my mood?

Does this belief help me to think productively and to act appropriately?[2]

If we are successfully disputing, the answer to these questions will be "no, no where, there is no evidence, or none." Remember the two important words: **PROVE IT!** Whatever our beliefs are, it is important to look for the facts and the proof before we choose to maintain the beliefs.

Suggested Homework for Chapter Four:

Take a least three of the specific irrational beliefs that you identified in Chapter Three. Now, put these beliefs on trial! Forcefully, actively, and passionately challenge the beliefs, using the various types of disputations and debates discussed in this chapter.

For the first irrational belief that you identified, use logical disputes in order to challenge and change the belief.

Now use empirical disputes to attack the second irrational belief.

Finally use practical or pragmatic disputations for the third irrational belief.

Also remember that just because we think a particular way doesn't make it factually correct. I can believe all day long that my table is a dog, but my thinking this way doesn't make it so. And I can prefer for people to treat me kindly, but there is no such universal law. If there was such a law, people indeed would always treat each other kindly and fairly.

CHAPTER FIVE

Getting the Sharks Back in the Cages

In Chapter Four, I talked about disputing underlying irrational beliefs. In this chapter, I want to look at some of the specific types of "irrational belief" sharks that can swim around in our lives and create problems.

In this chapter, you will learn more about specific disputation techniques, and also how to replace your irrational beliefs with rational alternatives.

Depression Sharks

One of the most common types of emotional upset is **depression**. Many of the people that I see in therapy complain of feeling depressed. Depression is different from feeling sad, blue, or down in the dumps. People can feel depressed for extended periods of time (longer than two weeks), and often experience changes in their appetite with resulting weight gain or loss, have trouble sleeping, have very little energy, may be agitated, feel worthless, and have difficulty thinking or concentrating. During these periods of depression, there may even be thoughts of suicide. [1]

It has been my experience that when people feel significantly depressed, the irrational belief sharks that are swimming around have to do with self-directed shoulds (musts, shoulds, and demands about the self) as well as the tendency to engage in self-damning and self-downing.

Let's go back to the person I mentioned earlier who made the mistake at work. This man was feeling quite depressed, and he and I were able to uncover a number of core irrational beliefs. First, he believed that he must never make mistakes at work, and that if he did make a mistake, this meant that he was a failure.

How would you get this shark back in its cage?

Starting with the belief that he must never make a mistake, it would be important for him to challenge this belief in a number of ways. Empirically, where is the evidence that says this man, or any human being, must never make mistakes? Is it logical to believe that any human will be able to avoid making mistakes at home, at work, or elsewhere? What are the consequences of believing that we must never make a mistake? Maintaining this belief might help us in the short run to be more conscientious and avoid making mistakes, but holding onto this belief in the long run will result in our putting tremendous pressure on ourselves.

This man would frequently say in therapy, "I shouldn't have made the mistake!" And I would ask, "Why not?" I would encourage him to write down the reasons why he believed it would be a good idea and preferable not to make mistakes, as well as the evidence for the belief that he must not make mistakes. While there was a great deal of evidence supporting his preference for avoiding mistakes, there was absolutely no evidence supporting the dogmatic, absolutistic command that he must not make mistakes. By the very fact that we are FMHB's (Fallible, Messed-up Human Beings), there is all the evidence in the world to support that we will make mistakes.

Now let's look at the second part of this man's belief. He believed that not only should he never make mistakes, but also that if he did make mistakes, he was a failure. Imagine for a moment that you had a friend who has this belief, or perhaps that you're a therapist working with a client who holds onto this way of thinking. Write down specific questions that you would use in order to challenge and debate this irrational belief:

IT'S NOT AS BAD AS IT SEEMS

Would you point out to this person the differences between rational and irrational beliefs? Would you point out that one set of beliefs is helpful and the other is hurtful? Vividly imagine that you maintain the belief that you must never make a mistake, and that if you do, you're a failure, and see what happens when you apply the disputations to these beliefs.

In challenging the belief that, "I am a failure because I made a mistake," it would be important to use both empirical and logical forms of disputing. What evidence is there to support the belief that just because we fail at certain things (which we surely do!), we are therefore failures as human beings? There is no evidence at all to support this idea, since being human means we will fail at many different things. As we discussed earlier, in order to be a failure as a person, it would be necessary to evaluate each of our millions of characteristics, traits, and actions, and conclude, beyond a shadow of a doubt, that each of these characteristics were 100 percent rotten failures. Is it logical to conclude that failing at something will suddenly turn our essence and personhood into a total failure?

We know of several examples in the New Testament in which it is reported that Jesus became quite angry and even acted, perhaps, badly. Does this mean that because he failed to maintain control over his anger in those situations, he was a failure? Albert Schweitzer, Mother Theresa, Joan of Arc, and other people known for their great deeds have surely failed in certain situations. But, these failures, and our own failures, even if they are rather significant failures, do not add up to the conclusion that we as humans are total failures.

As we forcefully challenge these irrational beliefs and learn that there is no support for them, we then recognize the importance of changing our irrational beliefs to rational beliefs. If the absolutistic commandment, "I must never make mistakes" is an irrational belief, and if this belief cannot be supported, then what is the rational alternative?

A rational alternative belief is based on wants, wishes, and preferences. A preference might be, "I wish I hadn't made that mistake at work, and I did, and it only proves that I'm human. It's too bad that I made the mistake, but it's not the end of the world." The

5 6

rational alternative would conclude that "I may fail at things, but failing at things does not make me a failure as a person!"

When people have maintained irrational beliefs for a long time, the replacement of these beliefs with rational alternatives often seems fake and phony. People often complain that they're just "faking it." In Alcoholics Anonymous, there is an expression, "Fake it till you make it!" Sometimes, when we begin to change underlying irrational beliefs, it is necessary to fake it until these beliefs start taking hold and become more deeply ingrained. When I first took French in high school and German in college, the phrases that I learned seemed quite fake and unnatural. But with practice, these words and sentences became more and more natural, and eventually I found myself dreaming in the language I was studying.

Let's say you're the therapist, and you've been helping this man who believes he's a failure because he made a mistake at work. You've been through the disputation process. The man recognizes that there is no law that says he must never make mistakes, and that he is not a failure just because he fails at things. However, he complains that he still feels depressed.

What this means is that despite passionate efforts at disputation, there still remains a shark that is loose and swimming around. It means that it is important to start looking again for underlying irrational beliefs that may have been missed initially. Chances are, if the man is still feeling depressed, he is still intensely "shoulding on" himself and "damning" himself (not his actions) for his mistakes. There may be some "silent shoulds" still swimming around that have not yet been detected and challenged.

As you practice these techniques, I encourage you to recognize that you are a human. I warn you not to become disheartened when your initial efforts seem unsuccessful. It will require continuous work and practice to identify the underlying irrational beliefs associated with the undesirable emotional and behavioral consequences, and to challenge and dispute these irrational beliefs.

Dr. Ellis has often quoted Oscar Wilde, who said, "Anything worth doing is worth doing badly!" As you first began detecting and debating irrational beliefs, chances are you may be less than 100 percent successful. Again, this doesn't make you a failure as a human being, but simply means you failed to accurately detect and effectively dispute the underlying irrational beliefs.

Anxiety Sharks

Recent evidence has suggested that people in the United States suffer more from anxiety-related problems than from any other problems, including depression.[2]

When we speak of **anxiety**, we are not referring to a mild concern or appropriate fear associated with a potentially dangerous situation. We are talking about excessive or unrealistic worry and anxiety that lasts for long periods of time, accompanied by symptoms such as trembling, muscle tension, restlessness, shortness of breath, palpitations, sweating, dizziness, and feeling "on edge."

People who experience panic attacks often complain of having a surge of anxiety and state that these attacks occur quite frequently. They, too, complain of having shortness of breath, dizziness, palpitations, sweating, trembling, choking sensations, feelings of tingling or numbness, chest pain, and beliefs that they are perhaps dying or going crazy. The intensity, duration, and frequency of these symptoms make them quite problematic.

Some people think that all anxiety is bad, and this is not the case. In fact, if we did not have at least mild degrees of concern and anxiety, we would probably not accomplish many of the goals that we set for ourselves. For example, if students didn't feel at least mildly anxious about upcoming tests, they probably wouldn't study. On the other hand, if they felt intensely anxious or had frequent panic attacks, they would most likely not be able to study because of the debilitating anxiety. If we don't have reasonable concern about the possibility of traffic accidents, we probably wouldn't pay attention to our own driving and to the drivers around us. So, our goal is not to eliminate appropriate concern and anxiety, but to eliminate those intense feelings of anxiety, nervousness, tension, and panic that get in our way of finding and maintaining happiness.

What are anxiety sharks like, and how do we put them back in their cages? Anxiety sharks are almost always based on the tendency to awfulize, catastrophize, and terribleize. We begin to "what if," and before we know it, we have ourselves worked into a frenzy. Certain thinking errors discussed earlier often occur here, including jumping to conclusions and fortune-telling, overgeneralization, magnification, and all-or-nothing thinking.

When I initially made the decision to go into the full-time, independent practice of clinical psychology, I experienced a considerable amount of appropriate concern and trepidation. However, I could have taken this appropriate concern and quickly escalated it into inappropriate anxiety. For example, I could have started with, "What if people don't come to see me?" From here, I could have quickly moved to awfulizing, such as, "If people don't come to see me, I won't have any clients, I won't have any income, and that would be absolutely awful!" I would then begin to predict failure, which could trigger even more catastrophizing and awfulizing.

Once again, think of yourself as a therapist. You have just listened to this client complain of feeling extremely anxious, you've identified the activator as his decision to go into private practice, and you have identified the likely core irrational belief as awfulizing. How would you start disputing this irrational thinking? Would you agree that the belief is indeed irrational? Some people might feel that it's not irrational to think that it would be awful if the person was unsuccessful in developing his or her profession. Well, let's check it out and see.

Using challenges such as, "Would it indeed be awful, 100 percent bad, if you were unable to develop your private practice?" I might respond that it would be indeed extremely bad if I didn't develop my practice, because I wouldn't have any income, I might lose my house, my car, and other material possessions. What would be your response as a therapist?

IT'S NOT AS BAD AS IT SEEMS

Hopefully, you would point out that indeed it would be bad, even quite bad, if these events did happen. But there is a big distinction between "bad" and "awful." You might ask if these events would be the worst thing imaginable. Would a private practice collapsing be worse than a family member developing a fatal disease? Would it be worse than a tornado striking the neighborhood? When disputing awfulizing, it is important to remember that there is always a degree of badness. And, no matter how bad certain things may be, it is unlikely that any of these events would in fact be 100 percent bad.

I personally believe that some things are indeed very, very bad. For example, I believe that when children are physically or sexually abused, it's one of the worst things that I can imagine. But I realize that no matter how bad a child may be mistreated, there are always examples (some quite shocking) of worse treatment. If I were to define such abuse as "awful," it would make it very difficult for me to work effectively with individuals who have been abused or mistreated. My belief that such mistreatment was "awful" would likely interfere with my concentration, and could result in my feeling extremely anxious every time I thought about their specific abuse, or I might choose to simply "whine" along with or pity people who have had very bad experiences. If I did any of these things, how helpful could I be?

As I have mentioned several times, rational thinking does not mean eliminating emotions, white-washing events, or thinking positively. I do not "think positively" about child physical or sexual abuse. Further, every time I hear of such abuse, I feel intensely sad and appropriately angry about such abuse. But these feelings and thoughts help rather than hinder.

To review, the specific disputations used in order to put our anxiety sharks back in their cages include the following questions:

While the event or anticipated event might be bad, could it really be 100 percent bad?

If you believe that something is 100 percent bad, are you then saying that there is nothing else in the entire world that could possibly be worse than this?

60

IT'S NOT AS BAD AS IT SEEMS

It may be difficult to change your thinking in this area. For a long time, you may have believed that certain things indeed were 100 percent (or 101 percent) bad, but what have been the consequences of maintaining these beliefs? Practically speaking, if we engage in anti-awfulizing, and reduce our levels of intense anxiety and panic, we become better able to problem-solve and handle situations including those "really bad" situations.

Panic Sharks

The panic shark deserves special comment. When people experience **panic disorders**, they almost always experience certain physical sensations and begin to engage in what has been called **"catastrophic misinterpretation."**[3]

These are the physical sensations that tend to activate thoughts such as, "Oh my goodness, here it comes again, I'm going to have another panic attack! These panic attacks are awful, and I just can't bear them! Maybe these attacks prove that I'm losing my mind! Or, maybe I'm going to have a heart attack and die!" Throughout this process, people are also prone to hyperventilate, which results in a buildup of carbon dioxide, which only makes the sensations of anxiety and panic even worse.

Panic sharks are best dealt with by learning to recognize the physical sensations. Once recognized, it is important to breathe deeply, in through the nose and out through the mouth. While breathing deeply, you can challenge the irrational belief that "This is awful!" by reminding yourself that the sensation is just that, a physical sensation, which can be understood and tolerated.

Alternative rational beliefs can also be used, such as, "While the sensations that I have are uncomfortable and I surely don't like them, the feelings aren't unbearable, and I won't die or go crazy." Although we may awfulize about the sensations, to the best of my knowledge, no one has ever died from experiencing a panic attack.

Further, having a panic attack is not an indication of "going crazy" but rather of a problem area that can be changed. If, however, the belief is that the sensations are absolutely awful and terrible, these thoughts will feed the fire of anxiety and panic.

Anger Sharks

Irrational beliefs that create **anger** are associated with many different types of problems. Not only is there the intensely uncomfortable feeling of anger, but people who feel such anger and rage often engage in behaviors that are equally as destructive. I have heard many stories about angry people putting their hands through walls, destroying property, kicking the side of a car, cussing out a boss and getting fired, or hitting another person, resulting in criminal charges being placed.

As we have discussed, anger comes from musturbation. People dogmatically and in a godlike fashion maintain the belief that certain people, places, and things must be different than what, in fact, they are. They dogmatically hold onto these commands despite serious consequences.

Sometimes, anger is used to conceal other underlying emotions, such as depression and anxiety. Anger may be used to conceal feelings of inadequacy and insecurity, and in these cases, the anger might be thought of as **"self-worth" anger**.[4] The person may maintain the irrational belief that other people must treat them the way they want to be treated, which results in feelings of anger. However, beneath this belief is the thought, "But if I were somehow a better person, people would treat me the way I want to be treated. Therefore, I must be a failure!"

Let's deal with "simple" anger first. When was the last time that you felt really angry?

Look for the underlying demand, commandment, and musturbation associated with this anger. Now, use the disputation techniques.

Where is the evidence for the belief? Is it logical that because you believe life must be a particular way or a person must behave the way you want, that it must therefore be that way? Pragmatically, what is the benefit from maintaining the belief that this person, place, or thing must be any particular way?

As somebody once asked me many years ago, "Who died and made you God?" If we're feeling intensely angry, then the chances are that we are playing God and insisting that what we think suddenly should become reality.

If people did, in fact, believe the way we did in all situations, perhaps the world would be a better place. For example, it would be nice if all people treated all other people fairly. It would be nice if people didn't kill or steal from other people.

But if we take these preferences and elevate them to absolutistic commandments based on shoulds and musts, then the problems occur. Our anger-creating shark gets out of the cage and swims gleefully around. It is important to remind ourselves that just because we would want certain people to act differently, would want ourselves to act differently, and would want life conditions to be different, this hardly means that it *must* be.

You might be thinking something like, "But the Ten Commandments say that people shall not kill or rob!" That is certainly correct, and the Ten Commandments, as well as other teachings, serve as useful, moral guidelines and directives. However, unlike laws of gravity and other laws of physics, these are just guidelines and directives, they do not represent universal absolutes. As I have said, if they did represent absolutes, then people would not steal or kill, they would not commit adultery, and so on.

In disputing anger-creating irrational beliefs, we chip away at what we see as being our own absolute shoulds and musts. Other people are who they are and do what they do, and no matter how strongly we maintain our belief that they must not act that way, there is no connection between our belief and their actions. Reality is reality. Just because we don't like it doesn't meant it will change.

Successful disputing of anger sharks means that we replace the musts, oughts, and shoulds with **Preferential Thinking**. Instead of believing that people must treat us a certain way, we can develop the alternative belief that we would prefer that people would treat us a certain way. Then, when we are "mistreated" (which we surely will be), we will still feel irritated and annoyed, but these feelings will be quite appropriate and will not interfere with our ability to solve problems and find happiness.

As we discussed in Chapter Two, notice how successful disputing results in new **E's** and **F's**. The **Effects (E's)** of the disputing are our new rational beliefs that help to get the sharks back in their cages. The new **F's** are the **Feelings** of irritation or annoyance, replacing the intense feelings of anger and rage. As already mentioned, annoyance and irritation can help us to reach our Goals (G), whereas anger and rage only serve to block our efforts.

Frustration Sharks

Much of my life is spent in meetings. We have meetings at our office, meetings at the hospital, and meetings about meetings! Recently, during a particularly busy week, I had a meeting that was scheduled for 7 p.m. The time arrived for the meeting, and I arrived on time. Unfortunately, many of the other people scheduled to attend were not so prompt.

I found myself feeling increasing **Frustration** (emotional consequence). The frustration kept increasing in intensity until finally I recognized that my irrational belief shark, which creates frustration, had gotten loose and was swimming madly about.

At this point, I decided to apply the ABC's of RET to my own situation. I recognized that the emotional consequence was intense frustration and that the activator was people being late for a scheduled meeting. Now it was time to look for the irrational beliefs, and soon I realized that I was thinking, "I can't stand it when people are late for scheduled meetings!"

IT'S NOT AS BAD AS IT SEEMS

I couldn't stand it? That was several months ago, and yet I'm still alive today! Did I like what was happening? Heck, no. But, there is a big difference between believing that I don't like something and believing that I can't stand it. The belief that "I can't stand it" is clearly irrational because of its illogical nature and because maintaining the belief results in negative consequences that are self-, other- and relationship-defeating. So, what would the disputation techniques be?

I began by asking myself, "Is it true that I can't stand it when people are late for meetings?" Answer: No, it's not true. I can stand it, but I really don't like it when people are late. There was also a "should" in there, that people should be prompt for meetings, just like I am. The disputation question for this belief is, "Where is it written that just because you're on time for meetings, other people must absolutely be on time as well?" Answer: Nowhere! I can be on time because I view this as being important, but other people may not have the same priorities that I have.

If I couldn't stand people being late for meetings, then I would die instantly on the spot. But I didn't die, so there is more proof that I can stand it, even though I don't like it.

Early in my professional career, I worked with children who had various types of psychological difficulties. I remember learning from someone at the Institute for Rational-Emotive Therapy the following jingle:

"I don't like it,
That's okay,
I can stand it
Anyway!"

I used to use this jingle a lot with children who found it quite helpful in dealing with situations in which they experienced intense frustration. Even today, when I feel frustrated, I will push this statement through my head, and find that my frustration level dramatically drops.

Even after successful disputation, I may still feel mild frustration and some degree of discomfort, but the intensity of these feelings is well within an appropriate and healthy range. The more forcefully that I remind myself that I can, indeed, stand anything (at least until it kills me!), the better able I am to keep my frustration shark in its cage. This doesn't mean that I will like what I am standing, but it does mean that I am more in control of my personal comfort level.

After I successfully disputed my "I-Can't-Stand-It-Itis," I developed the new, effective belief (rational belief) that I *could* stand it even though I didn't like it. My new feeling was still mild frustration, but at this reduced level, it was not defeating. Further, once I reduced my frustration, I was better able to use my time constructively, since there was a delay in the meeting. Rather than sitting around stewing and making myself incredibly frustrated, I was able to get some paperwork done.

Suggested Homework for Chapter Five:

Now that you have a better idea about the particular types of underlying irrational beliefs and methods for disputing these irrational beliefs, identify your own irrational beliefs that you would like to more forcefully dispute and change. Perhaps you can get some ideas from Chapter Four, in which you recorded some of your irrational beliefs or from the journal that you are keeping:

Write down the ABC's for a number of different emotional episodes. For example, if you found yourself feeling intensely angry, identify the emotional and behavioral consequence, the activator that preceded these feelings and actions, and the underlying irrational beliefs that created the anger.

Now, use the disputation techniques described in Chapters Four and Five. Use a number of different challenges, and be forceful and active in this disputation process. Use the outline below to complete this assignment. I recommend starting with consequences, moving to the activators, and then to the beliefs.

Consequences

What are the disturbed and inappropriate negative emotions that you felt, such as depression, rage, anger, anxiety, panic, frustration, etc.?

What were the inappropriate behaviors or actions that were self-, other-, and/or relationship-defeating?

Activators:

Describe what happened immediately before you started having the feelings and performing the actions described above. The activator can be actual events as well as feelings, anticipated events, or even memories.

IT'S NOT AS BAD AS IT SEEMS

Beliefs:

What are the irrational beliefs related to the activator above that cause the emotional and behavioral consequences?

Disputation:

Now that you've detected your irrational beliefs, it's time to start putting these beliefs and attitudes "on trial" in your psychological court of law. Remember, these beliefs are tested by looking for proof and facts to support the attitudes. Where's the evidence that supports my belief? Where is it written (other than in my personal book of rules)? Can I prove my belief beyond a shadow of a doubt? Is there an universal law (like the law of gravity) that would back up my belief? Is my belief logical? Is my belief helping me to reach my goals and achieve reasonable happiness?

Continue disputing until your anger, for example, has been changed to mild annoyance or irritation. If the intensity of the feelings do not change, continue to look for underlying irrational beliefs which may not have been uncovered. Use the vertical arrow technique as well as other methods discussed in order to seek out the irrational belief. Keep challenging and disputing.

Effects of Disputing:

Once you've been successful in disputing the underlying irrational beliefs, you have now developed new **Rational Beliefs**. These are the logical, preferential (wanting, wishing, and desiring rather than requiring and demanding), flexible, and self-, other-, and relationship-enhancing beliefs and attitudes that help reach goals and achieve our purpose in life. What are the new rational beliefs that you developed?

Feelings:

What are the new feelings and behaviors/actions that you accomplished after successfully disputing and developing rational beliefs? Remember, after successful debating of irrational beliefs, you won't necessarily feel good! The goal is to eliminate inappropriate, negative emotions such as depression, guilt, anger, panic, and intense frustration and replace these with appropriate negative feelings such as regret, disappointment, sadness, concern, annoyance, etc.

It is important to do this written homework so that you can review and perhaps find some areas in which you can improve in the disputation process. Remember, if you're not successful, it doesn't make you a failure as a human being, but simply provides you with another opportunity to apply effective thinking straight skills.

CHAPTER SIX

"I Feel Like Pond Scum!" :
The Story of Ruth

So far, we've talked about outlook. We've learned that it's not external events that "make" us happy, but rather our outlook concerning those events.

We've discussed the specific types of "stinking thinking" that create emotional upset like depression, anxiety, anger, and frustration. We've learned how to manage and eliminate emotional disturbance by applying the Rational-Emotive Therapy debating techniques and the ABC's of Thinking Straight, which are designed to change irrational beliefs into rational thoughts.

By now, you have begun to apply those "thinking straight" tools, and I hope you're seeing the benefits of rational thinking. Remember, the more homework you complete, and the more active you are in applying the skills you've learned, the greater the rewards and benefits!

But if you're human like the rest of us, I suspect that you probably haven't always been able to apply the "thinking straight" techniques and principles. And you may have even wondered, "Does this stuff really work?"

Since I see many people each week in individual, couples, family, and group therapy, I know it works, because I get to see the results - the new patterns of thinking, feeling, and behaving, and the elimination of emotional turmoil and disturbance. But I have often wished that people who have never been in therapy or counseling could be "flies on the wall" and hear what actually goes on behind the closed doors of therapy. Of course, what goes on in therapy is protected by confidentiality, and this fortunately keeps all the "flies" off the walls!

One day as I was working on this book, I mentioned to my wife, Christy, that I wished there was some way I could give people a better idea about how "thinking straight" therapy really worked.

"Couldn't you take bits and pieces from different therapy sessions," Christy asked, "and disguise them in order to protect confidentiality, then work them into fictional therapy sessions? Then you could really demonstrate how RET helps clients cope with depression, anger, anxiety, and other problems."

And that's what I'm going to do in the next few chapters. I'll occasionally "stop" the imaginary session, discuss what's going on, and ask you to imagine yourself as the therapist. You can decide what you would do, then see how it coincides with what actually happens in the session.

Ruth - The First Session

Ruth* was a 27-year-old single woman who, to most people, would seem to "have it all." She was intelligent, attractive, and successful in her job. She had recently bought a nice condominium, was saving money, and had good friends.

So, why would Ruth seek therapy? Let's become those "flies on the wall" and listen in on the first session:

EN: (That's me) So, Ruth, tell me about the problems that you're having that motivated you to come see me today.

Well, you know, I'm not really sure. I told one of my friends that I was thinking about getting into therapy, and she looked at me as if I had two heads or something. "You've got it made," she told me. She even laughed and said that she wished she had it as bad as I did! That's part of the problem, I guess. I do have all the trappings of happiness. I have a good job, a nice car, a new condo, friends

---

*   Remember, informations has been significantly changed in order to protect confidentiality. Any resemblance to persons living or dead is purely coincidental.

and family who love me. But even with all of this, I'm miserable. I really am depressed, and I've felt depressed for a long time. I had always wanted to get my own place, and I thought once I got the condo I would start to feel better. It didn't work. In fact, I've felt even a little more depressed since I bought the place a few months ago.

EN: On a 0-to-10-point scale, with 0 being "not at all" and 10 and 10 being being "the most severely and extremely depressed possible," where would you put your depression today?

As I've mentioned in earlier chapters, I like to have people "anchor" their feelings, that is, put a number on the level of depression. I use a "Daily Mood Record"[1] (see Appendix) so my clients and I can not only measure the levels of emotions, but also, and more importantly, see the change that takes place.

R: An 8 or 9 at least. Sometimes I can't sleep very well, I don't concentrate at work like I should be able to, and I just don't enjoy the things I used to.

EN: So, the feelings of depression have really been getting in your way. And it sounds to me like the depression has been pretty long-standing and the intensity is a lot more than just feeling sad.

R: (Interrupts) Oh, definitely! I've felt sad before, and what I feel now is much, much different than feeling sad. I mean, I felt sad when my grandmother died a few years ago. I felt sad when the deal fell through on the first condo I wanted. Then I felt sad. And there's a big difference between feeling sad and what I feel now. Don't get me wrong, I'm not going to kill myself or anything. But these feelings are the pits. If you want to use a 10-point scale, then I feel at least an 8, and probably closer to a 9.

Had Ruth not volunteered her thoughts of suicide, I would have asked, and I did ask many more specific questions during the first session. When people feel depressed, their thinking is often so crooked that suicide becomes an option that they think about

72

frequently. But suicide is **never** a good option. If you have friends who have told you they feel depressed, don't be afraid to ask them about suicidal thoughts and encourage them to call a mental health professional (psychologist, psychiatrist, social worker, counselor, etc.) immediately.

At this stage, I am continuing to get a handle on the problem that Ruth has. I want to be as specific as possible, especially when we talk about emotions. English is very imprecise when we talk about feelings. What is called "depression" by one person might be considered merely "sadness" by another. I want to make sure that Ruth and I are speaking the same language, and that I understand as best I can how she is feeling.

In Rational-Emotive Therapy, and other forms of cognitive-behavior therapy, we like to measure change based on intensity, duration, and frequency rather than on the presence or absence of negative emotions and behaviors. While the goal will be to eliminate Ruth's depression, if that is the problem, I'll want to teach her that in the future she may feel mildly depressed again, but that she will be able to manage the intensity, duration, and frequency of these episodes in a healthy fashion. As I said in Chapter Two, one of the goals of RET is to recognize the difference between appropriate negative emotions (e.g., sorrow, disappointment, etc.) which come from rational thinking (wanting, wishing, preferring philosophies) and inappropriate negative emotions (depression, anger, rage, and anxiety) which develop when we start musturbating and absolutistically demanding that people (including ourselves) and life conditions be different than in fact they are.

The first session continues, and I ask various questions in an effort to gain a better understanding of the problem Ruth is presenting. After talking for some time, Ruth and I have agreed that one of the goals of therapy will be to eliminate her depression. We have identified the undesirable emotional consequence (depression) and now I will want to look for problematic actions or behaviors that are related to the depression.

EN: It certainly sounds like you have been feeling depressed. When you feel depressed, what do you usually do?

R: Usually, nothing. I may watch television, but I don't really enjoy it. Sometimes I eat something, but I'm afraid I'm going to put on weight and I usually end up feeling guilty for having eaten something. Some of my friends have told me to call them, but I don't, because I know I'll just bring them down or bore them with my problems. I'd like to get out more, you know, to go out on dates or something, but I'll just end up getting hurt.

In Chapter Three, we talked about specific types of "thinking errors" such as overgeneralization, mental filter, and emotional reasoning. Put your "therapist hat" on and see if you can identify some of the thinking errors that Ruth is making that may be related to her depressed mood. List them below:

If you said "jumping to conclusions," I agree. She seems to be acting as if she has a crystal ball and can predict the future (fortune-telling). She negatively predicts that she "will" bore her friends or bring their moods down. She is also predicting that if she goes out on dates, she'll "just end up getting hurt."

My guess is that as our sessions progress, we'll find some other very specific types of underlying irrational beliefs and thinking errors. Based on what you have read in previous chapters, what types of "stinking thinking" do you think we'll find? What type of sharks do you think are swimming around in Ruth's ocean? Keep your therapist hat on and write your guesses below.

EN: When you feel depressed, you tend to avoid opportunities and situations that could potentially be pleasurable, right?

IT'S NOT AS BAD AS IT SEEMS

Yeah. It's just easier to sit home and be a vegetable than to get off my rear and do something.

We are making progress in identifying both the emotional and behavioral consequences (the C's). The self-defeating emotion is depression. The undesirable behavioral consequence is avoidance.

Avoidance is a self-defeating behavioral consequence experienced by many people who feel depressed. Avoidance can be related to other symptoms of depression such as lack of energy, negative self-concept, and certain thinking errors. It can also be related to the "security of misery versus the misery of insecurity." In other words, depression and avoidance can become bad habits that are maintained in some cases simply "because it's easier."

Sometimes when I've felt a little depressed, angry, or frustrated, I've known what to do, but just didn't feel like doing it. Why? Well, it's almost like having an old pair of shoes with holes in them. If I wear them when it's raining, my feet get wet. I could just throw the old shoes away and wear other shoes. But these old shoes are *SO COMFORTABLE*. I just hate to break in new shoes! My feet may hurt! So, I just stay in my "comfort zone" and keep wearing my old shoes. It's not that I'm lazy, or don't want to wear new shoes. I do. It's just that my underlying irrational beliefs and thinking errors get in the way. I might predict that the new shoes will never fit as well as the old shoes. I might predict that my feet will hurt, or that people won't like my new shoes.

Depression and avoidance are often like the old shoes. People grow accustomed to and comfortable with what they know best. These people are not being lazy, and they certainly don't like feeling depressed! Sometimes they even get depressed about being depressed! (Ruth does this, as you'll see later.) This can make the depression worse. In some types of depression, biological changes take place that can almost paralyze the person and make it nearly impossible to exert any energy at all. (If this is the case, a referral to a psychiatrist would be in order, to determine whether medication might be necessary as part of the therapy.)

In Ruth's case, the evaluation sessions and psychological testing that were completed did not suggest the type of depression

75

that would respond to medication. Also, she told me that she really didn't want to be on medicine. Instead, her depression and avoidance seemed to be related to her patterns of unhealthy, irrational thinking.

An important part, if not the most important part, of therapy is the partnership between the therapist and the client. One ingredient of this partnership is an agreement on the problems and goals of therapy. Without a definition of the problems and an agreement on the goals, therapy might be like going on vacation without ever agreeing on where you want to go. You might get in your car with your family or friends and drive for a week or two, but never arrive anywhere because you didn't know where you were going in the first place.

One of the nicest things about the Rational-Emotive Therapy "thinking straight approach" is that there is agreement on the vacation destination city! The first two goals that Ruth and I agreed on were to eliminate her defeating levels of depression and to replace her avoidance behavior with more active, self- and relationship-enhancing actions.

EN: Ruth, we've agreed that you want to work on getting rid of your depression and becoming a more active participant in life, rather than being a passive observer who just sits at home watching television, dreaming of what might be. Even though you mentioned that you've felt depressed for several years, I'm wondering if you can think of anything that has recently happened that might be related to your feeling depressed right now.

R: Like what?

EN: Well, sometimes people experience certain stressors in their lives that can tend to trigger greater levels of personal distress. Examples include negative events like increased financial burdens, deaths of friends or family members, or changes in relationships. But positive events like a job promotion or the birth of a child can also activate a depressed mood.

R: I hadn't really thought much about it, but now that you mention it, Bob and I did break up about a month ago.

EN: Bob?

R: Yeah. Bob was a guy I had been dating for several months. I didn't think about it when we first started talking today, since it really doesn't seem like a big deal. I mean, it was no surprise. I date a guy a while, and he usually ends up dumping me. And besides, I was feeling depressed before he broke up with me.

EN: Was there any change in your level of depression?

R: If I'm honest, I guess there was. While we were dating, I was feeling good. Good for me, anyway! Do you want me to use that 10-point scale?

EN: Yes, that would help.

R: Even when Bob and I were going out, I still felt depressed, but only about a 6. When he dropped the bombshell on me that he wanted to end the relationship, that really made me depressed!

I wanted to see if there were any specific A's (activators) related to Ruth's depression. With a little exploration, she was able to identify a recent event that may have served to trigger her current depression. So, we now have the C's (emotional and behavioral consequences) and the A (activator).

It's time to put on your therapist hat again. What would you guess I'm going to do now? Write your ideas below:

R: Ruth, you said that when Bob broke up with you, that really made you depressed. What exactly did you mean?

R: Well, for me, I was doing okay. But, when he told me he just wanted to be friends and didn't want to go out anymore, that's what really got me depressed.

EN: So, you're saying that when Bob broke up with you, that *made* you more depressed.

R: Exactly.

EN: I like to think of therapy as being an educational process that teaches people to be their own scientists and therapists. As scientists, you and I will want to test out certain ideas and see if they are reasonable and objective. Would you be willing to start the "thinking like a scientist" process now?

R: Sure, why not?

EN: When you said that you got more depressed when Bob broke up with you, that means that it was the breakup that controlled your feelings.

R: Right.

EN: In Rational-Emotive Therapy, or RET, you'll learn a new set of ABC's designed to help you eliminate your depression. The **A** stands for the activator, meaning the event or even the memory that you experience just before you begin to feel depressed. I'm going to skip the **B** for now. The **C** stands for emotional consequences, your feelings and behavioral consequences, what you actually do when you feel depressed. So, **A** stands for activator and **C** stands for consequences. Okay?

R: Okay.

EN: EN: For you, the A in this situation is Bob's ending the dating relationship, and the C is your feeling 8 or 9 depressed and avoiding potentially healthy situations.

R: So far, that makes sense.

EN: You're saying that **A** caused **C**, right?

R: Sure. If Bob hadn't dumped me, I wouldn't have gotten so depressed. So of course, the activator or whatever you call it made me depressed.

EN: When you were in high school, did you date much?

R: As a matter of fact, I did. In high school I was pretty popular. I was even in the homecoming court once.

EN: So you maybe dated every now and then.

R: I dated a lot. So what's your point?

EN: Did you ever break up with someone who really liked you?

R: (Laughing) Yeah, a bunch of times! Is it pay-back time or something?

EN: No, not at all. I'm just wondering. When you broke up with these guys, how did they react?

R: A couple of guys didn't miss a beat. They just asked somebody else out the next weekend. One guy was pretty hurt. I remember a boy named Fred who got really angry with me and told people in my class lies about me.

EN: Did guys ever break up with you in high school?

R: Of course they did.

EN: And how did you feel when it happened?

R: I don't know. Sometimes it bothered me, and sometimes it didn't. Mostly, I just waited for somebody else to ask me out.

EN: So, you didn't always react the same way?

R: Right.

EN: Did you ever feel a 9 depressed, stay home, watch TV, and swear you would never go out again?

IT'S NOT AS BAD AS IT SEEMS

R: No. But I don't get your point.

EN: If A caused C, or in this case, if a breakup of a dating rela-
       tionship caused depression, then would't it make any sense
       that every time you broke up with someone they would have
       gotten depressed? If A caused C, Fred would have gotten
       depressed, not angry. In fact, he would have been a 9 de-
       pressed. And if A caused C, when you were in high school
       and some guy broke up with you, you would have

R: No, it's different!

EN: Well, let's see. If A equals C, or activators cause conse-
       quences, then wouldn't it make sense that when A happens,
       everybody will react the same way and experience the same
       consequence?

R: But they don't. And besides, I still don't see how this
       relates to me.

EN: I want to test the idea that A equals C, that events control us
       and make us have certain feelings. What if I created a great
       new invention called the "kick machine." My kick machine
       is very sophisticated and I can set it to kick people in the
       shins. Once it's set, it always delivers the same amount of
       kick pressure to each person it kicks. My machine is an A.

R: So?

EN: I take my kick machine to a room with 25 people lined up. I
       move down the line and my kick machine kicks each person.
       Remember, the intensity of the kick is controlled so that each
       person will get exactly the same amount of force with each
       kick. Will every person react the same way?

R: No.

EN: You're exactly right! But, why not?

R: They're different. They have different personalities.

EN: Again, you're quite correct. But, pretend that I'm from Mars and help me to understand how come each of these humans reacted differently to the kick machine. Or, better yet, tell me how come people react differently to the end of loving or, at least, close relationships?

R: I don't know, except they're just different.

EN: If you go into an ice cream shop, what flavor ice cream will you order?

R: Probably strawberry. I really like strawberry.

EN: Not me. I'll order coffee ice cream.

R: Yuck. I hate coffee ice cream.

EN: Are you telling me that there is something wrong with coffee ice cream? (Laughing) Them's fightin' words!

R: No, I just said I didn't like it.

EN: Why don't you like it if there's nothing wrong with it?

R: I don't know. I just don't. I never have liked it.

EN: But, why don't you like it?

R: I just like strawberry better. I have just never had a taste for coffee ice cream.

EN: Oh, so you're saying that strawberry ice cream is not necessarily better or worse than coffee, it's just that you prefer strawberry. That your tastes may be different from mine, and mine different from yours. Right?

R: Yes.

EN: So how do you think the kick machine and ice cream relate to relationships ending and your feeling depressed?

IT'S NOT AS BAD AS IT SEEMS

R: Are you saying that it's not the event or the activator that makes us feel bad, but rather our tastes?

EN: That's almost exactly what I'm saying. People who have been dumped react differently. If the kick machine actually existed, people kicked by it would react differently. People like and dislike different foods and flavors of ice cream. These differences at point C are not caused by the As, but are related to the different tastes, preferences, perceptions, attitudes, and beliefs that people have. And that brings us to the B that I left out earlier. The B stands for beliefs that we have about all the different As that happen in our lives. There's nothing inherently right or wrong with coffee or strawberry ice cream. It's just my preferences and beliefs that I hold about these foods. I hated asparagus when I was a child, but today I love it! Has asparagus changed? No, just my tastes and preferences have changed. Epictetus said that "people are disturbed not by things but by the views they hold of them" and Shakespeare wrote in *Hamlet*, "It is neither good nor bad, but thinking makes it so." When those boys broke up with you in high school, you didn't feel the way you do today after Bob broke up with you, because you are thinking differently now than you did back then. Those were still relationships that you didn't want to end. But your attitudes, beliefs, and self-statements were different then and now. Does this make sense?

R: Yeah, it's starting to. You're saying that it's not what actually happens, but what happens in my head, that determines how I feel. Is that right?

EN: You're right on the money, Ruth. You are learning one of the most important lessons in this RET thinking straight approach to change. It's called the B-C Connection or Belief-Consequence Connection. You rarely if ever have control over the activators, such as events, or the actions of other people. But, you do have control, and will learn to have more control, over your BELIEFS about these events or actions. While you may be powerless over your A's, you will never be powerless over your B's. When you were in high school and somebody broke up with you, you didn't upset yourself over it. Maybe you just accepted that reality

82

and looked forward to future relationships. But when Bob broke off the dating relationship, you attached a whole different set of beliefs and attitudes to the event.

R: Boy, I'll say. I'm certainly not thinking about future relationships, other than to think that they'll fail just like the other ones have. I'm thinking that there must be something wrong with me. I'm just not the dating type, I'm a major failure, and I'm worse than all the pond scum on the lake behind my condo!

EN: Well, you're not, and we will be able to prove than beyond a shadow of a doubt! But, Ruth, it's going to take hard work and lots of practice. Each week I'm going to give you homework designed to teach you more about the B-C Connection and to help you uncover your underlying beliefs that are related to your depression and avoidance problems. This homework may be difficult and certainly will take time. Will you be willing to do it?

R: I'm sick of feeling depressed, so sure, I'll try.

EN: Try isn't good enough for me. Try is a passive verb. Watch me try and get out of my seat. (I then made a few half-hearted movements as I "tried" to get out of my seat.) Did I make it?

R: No.

EN: (With a whining voice) But Ruth, I tried!

R: (Laughs) So you mean it takes more than trying, it takes action.

EN: Yeah, it means working on changing, not trying or waiting for me or somebody else to change you. Your homework this week will be to keep a journal of your thoughts, feelings, and actions, and to keep your Daily Mood Record. Also, I want you to read several pamphlets by Dr. Ellis and Dr. Beck.[2,3,4]

IT'S NOT AS BAD AS IT SEEMS

This was the end of the first therapy session. Earlier I asked you to guess what I was going to do in the therapy session. Rather than starting to identify Ruth's specific underlying beliefs and attitudes, I wanted to teach her about the B-C Connection.

As I have emphasized repeatedly in this book, it's our beliefs that make the difference. Activators may contribute to our reactions, but it's our beliefs that cause the reactions in the long run.

Before you, me, or my clients can change, it is critical that we understand and accept that beliefs - not activators - cause emotional and behavioral consequences.

Ruth Goes Shark Hunting - The Second Session

A week later Ruth returned for her second therapy session. She had faithfully completed her Daily Mood Record and had read the pamphlets. I talked more about the ABC's of Rational-Emotive Therapy. (You may want to go back and review the ABC's right now in order to refresh your memory.)

We spent about ten minutes reviewing the homework and answering the questions she had about the material she had read. In reviewing her Daily Mood Record, it is obvious that Ruth had consistently felt a moderate level of depression during the entire week.

EN: Now Ruth, what would you like to accomplish during our session today?

R: I just wish that I could get a handle on my depression. I hate feeling the way I do! The stuff you had me read was good, and I understood it, but it didn't really help me much. As I read it, I realized that my problem is, I don't think positively enough. Isn't that what this therapy is going to be about, learning to think positively?

EN: Not really. In fact, while it's nice to be able to think positively about some things, I'm personally not much of an advocate of positive thinking. I mean, how are you supposed to "think positively" about Bob breaking up with

IT'S NOT AS BAD AS IT SEEMS

you? If you walked in here today and said you were feeling great because now you were thinking positively about the end of the relationship, I'd probably think that a little strange. Rather than pushing for positive thinking, I believe deeply and passionately in the "power of rational, non-negative thinking." But the first step in eliminating your depression is to figure out which of your beliefs caused your depression. From your Daily Mood Record, I see that you were a "9" depressed on Saturday. What was going on?

R: Nothing! Literally nothing! No date, no fun, no nothing. Plus, my television wasn't working, I called a couple of friends but they all had dates, even my cat didn't want to be around me. I felt so alone.

EN: How are you feeling right now as you're telling me about Saturday night?

R: Depressed.

EN: Yeah, you even sound depressed. What's going through you mind right now as you describe the evening for me?

What am I doing now with Ruth? I'm helping her to identify or uncover her underlying beliefs. She may have some understanding of how her beliefs largely cause her to feel what she feels, but she probably doesn't have a clue as to her specific types of "stinking thinking" that create her personal agony and depression. I might have some hunches, but I want to explore with Ruth in order to find her particular irrational beliefs and thoughts.

R: I just keep thinking about sitting there all alone.

EN: And what do you think about sitting there all alone?

R: I just feel lonely and depressed.

EN: Those are feelings, but what were the thoughts or statements you were making to yourself about being at home alone on Saturday night?

8 5

R: Like I said in my first session with you, I just keep thinking that there's something wrong with me. I'm not the dating type. I'm undesirable, like that scum on the pond.

I could test out these **"Automatic Assumptions"** about being "not the dating type" or somehow "undesirable." Based on our first session and the history she has given me, I am 99.9 percent certain that there is no evidence at all to support these inferential leaps. It would be worthwhile to do this, but right now I'm really more interested in detecting her core irrational beliefs. The automatic thoughts and inferences she presents provide clues needed to uncover the core iB (irrational belief).

So, for now, I'll pass on talking with her about her incorrect inferences and press on through the murky swamp of irrational thinking in search of the nasty, happiness-eating shark.

EN   Ruth, even though I don't believe this would ever happen, what if you didn't get a date for the next year or two? What would you think about yourself? What would it mean?

R: Gosh, that's a terrible thought! What would I think if I didn't get a date for a year or two? If I didn't get asked out for that long, I would know that there really is something wrong with me.

EN: If you didn't get asked out, that would prove there was something wrong with you. What would it prove was wrong with you? What would it say about you?

R: Everyone I know gets invited out, at least every now and then.

EN: So, if you didn't, then that would mean . . . . what?

R: I'm not the type of person that guys like to ask out.

EN: And, if that was true, in your mind and in your thinking about yourself, what would that say about you?

8 6

IT'S NOT AS BAD AS IT SEEMS

R: That I'm no good. That I'm a failure.

EN: I think you've just found one of those sharks we talked
        about. I smell the "I'm a failure" shark. And when you sat
        around Saturday night thinking that because you were at
        home alone and didn't have a date, you were a failure, you
        just kept feeling more and more depressed. Right?

R: Yeah, but if I would have had a date, then I wouldn't have
        felt depressed.

EN: Maybe, maybe not. But right now can you see how thinking
        to yourself, "I'm a failure . . . . I'm a failure . . . . I'm a
        failure . . . ." relates to feeling so depressed. If I go home
        tonight and start thinking that I'm a failure, pretty soon I'd
        feel depressed. Thinking of yourself as a failure, no good,
        or pond scum is what we refer to as self-downing or self-
        damning. It's like you are condemning the sinner (or the
        person) and not the sin (or the action.) It wouldn't surprise
        me if you've been self-rating like this for a long time.

R: I think you're right. I remember all the way through school,
        if I did badly on a test or on a homework assignment, I'd
        feel depressed for days. I'd think to myself, "You goof-
        ball! How could you be so stupid!"

EN: Exactly. Back then you were rating yourself a stupid person
        because you did poorly on a test. Today, you think you're a
        failure as a person if you happen to not have a date, for
        example. You rate yourself based on some type of external
        factor or event. If you have a date or do well on the test,
        you're good, wonderful, great, and happy. But, heaven
        forbid that you do poorly on a task or not have a date when
        you'd like to, because then you are rotten, miserable, and
        depressed - pond scum! Now we're getting somewhere.
        The shark of your depression sounds like self-rating and
        self-downing. If you want to play the "dating game" that's
        fine, but when you start playing the "rating game" watch
        out! You put your personhood on the line and begin to think

that your worth as a human is somehow magically connected to your social calendar, to your success at work, or to the number of dates you have per week or per year. When your value as a person gets tied to dates or other external "successes," then you start putting massive pressure on yourself. Guess what happens when you put so much pressure on yourself?

R: I know the answer to that one. I start trying too hard and usually end up blowing it somehow.

EN: That's right. It's like going to a dance and thinking repeatedly, "I must dance well, I must dance well," or driving down a road thinking, "I must not have a wreck." What do you think is going to happen?

R: You wouldn't be able to dance - or drive!

EN   Right, because you're placing demands on yourself and believing that if you fail at something, it makes you a failure. Ruth, does this seem to fit for you?

R: It really does. I've been self-critical for as long as I can remember. I have always been envious of people who can make a mistake or mess up, and just go on with life.

EN: How do you think their beliefs about themselves are different from yours?

R: I'm not sure.

EN: My guess is that they condemn the sin and not the sinner. They accept themselves as FMHBs, as Dr. Ellis says. They are able to rate and judge behaviors, actions, or characteristics without putting their so-called self-worth on the line. They recognize that mistakes and flaws are part of the human condition and that we are all imperfect. But you seem to command yourself that you must accomplish certain things or fit certain conditions, like have a date or a nice boyfriend, in order to view yourself as having worth as a person.

88

IT'S NOT AS BAD AS IT SEEMS

One of the beauties of the RET "thinking straight" approach to happiness is its simplicity in uncovering the sharks of irrational thinking. Certain forms of irrational thinking are associated with certain types of emotional upset and unhappiness.

In Chapter Three we discussed musturbation and its tendency to create anger; awfulizing, the "creator" of anxiety and panic; "I-Can't-Stand-It-Itis"; the shark of frustration problems; and "damnation," especially self-damning, that causes depression. Armed with this knowledge, you and I can begin to go on deep sea fishing trips in search of the elusive sharks of our unhappiness.

There's good news and bad news! The good news is that thanks to our newly found knowledge, we know just where to look for the sharks (for example, in Ruth's case, we know we are looking for the self-downing shark of depression). The bad news is that these sharks are big and powerful, and have usually been around for a long time. They've been cared for and fed well (by us, no less!), and while it's simple to find them, it's tough to get them back in their cages.

In my sessions with Ruth, we followed some specific steps, which you can follow to track down your sharks of unhappiness. First, we identified the problem (depression) and agreed on some goals (e.g., eliminating the depression). Second, we got more specific and looked for the emotional and behavioral Cs, the consequences. Third, we found the A, or activator, associated with the episode of depression.

Next, I emphasized the B-C Connection, that it's the beliefs that largely cause the emotional and behavioral consequences and not the events, situations, or other people. The B-C Connection is critically important to wellness, positive change, reaching the goals we set for ourselves, and resulting happiness. The B-C Connection gives us power, since we can control our thinking and can focus on changing our thinking rather than on trying to change other people, places, or things. That's why the B-C Connection is reviewed frequently throughout therapy, and specific irrational beliefs are firmly tied to the particular emotional and behavioral problems being presented.

IT'S NOT AS BAD AS IT SEEMS

At this stage, things get tough. We are now in the deep emotional and behavioral waters, hunting the sharks that have control. We know that Ruth's self-damning shark is down there. It's so powerful that when it swims around it creates all sorts of ripples, currents, and waves. It triggers Ruth's automatic thoughts and inferences such as, "I'll never be happy," "Nobody will ever want to date me," and "I'll always end up messing up somehow."

Remember, when the shark has been outside of its cage, swimming freely, Ruth has gone running for cover. This has created some of the behavioral responses or actions that are also self-, other-, and relationship-defeating. For example, because she predicts failure, she tends to avoid social opportunities that could potentially be rewarding. She also tends to overeat, and is certainly likely to put on weight. And although she emphatically denied any thoughts of hurting or killing herself, some people are more prone to harm themselves when the self-damning sharks are loose.

In order to get the depression shark back in its cage, I want to teach Ruth how to become a shark trainer and use effective shark repellant. As discussed in Chapter Four, shark trainers who are able to quickly round up the nasty sharks and get them back in their cages do so because they have developed the skills for disputing irrational beliefs.

Now it's time for Ruth to learn how to dispute the irrational belief we've identified so far.

R: So, what can I do?

EN: So far, we've covered the ABC's of Rational-Emotive Therapy, that is, the Activators, Beliefs, and Consequences. Now, it's time to move to the D's, or the Disputation. Ruth, do you remember talking about irrational beliefs as being sharks that swim in our emotional waters?

R: Yes.

EN: The first step is knowing that they're down there, but just knowing that isn't going to help much in reducing and eliminating your depression. When you are feeling depressed, it means that the sharks are in control and it's their territory, so to speak. Maybe I could avoid swimming where they are, but that wouldn't help me change my feelings. In order to take charge and find our happiness, we need to learn how to put the sharks back in protective cages and . . .

R: Kill 'em! Why can't we just learn how to kill 'em? If we just put them in cages, they could always get out again.

EN: You're right. Years ago I used to think that we could kill the sharks, and that was my goal as a therapist. But, as I have gotten older and maybe a little wiser I've learned that irrational thinking truly is a fact of life. If I could kill the irrational belief shark, then it would mean that I would NEVER think irrationally again, or feel and act inappropriately - ever again. How likely do you think that is?

R: It would be nice, but I guess it's not very realistic.

EN: For me, at least, it's not realistic at all. And I've worked at it! I have had many years of training in behavior therapy, Rational-Emotive Therapy, and cognitive-behavior therapy. As a therapist, I have the opportunity to practice my own "thinking straight" skills on a daily basis. I go to seminars and workshops, and I read books and write in my journal all the time. So, I guess that would mean that I will never feel or act in an inappropriate way.

R: Sounds good to me!

EN: Yeah, to me too. But, it doesn't work that way. Over the years I have increasingly been able to apply the skills I teach, and have reduced the intensity, duration, and frequency of certain problems. I have been able to build stronger and stronger cages for the sharks, and in fact, some of the sharks probably will stay safely locked in their cages. But, sometimes the salt water of stressors or other conditions corrode the cages, and a shark or two may get out. When that happens, I know they won't get me, because I'm trained. I use the disputation skills to get the sharks back in the cages. Are you ready to learn these shark trainer skills?

R: Am I ever.

EN: Good. When we first went over the ABC's, I mentioned that not only is there a Big D that stands for Disputation, but there are also three little ds. The first little d stands for **detecting**. Before we are able to change an irrational belief to a rational one, we need to know what the specific beliefs are. This is what we've done so far. You were able to identify that you often think of yourself as being a failure. The next little d stands for **discriminating**. We don't want to start debating and changing all of our beliefs. We have to discriminate between our rational and our irrational beliefs. Rational beliefs are positive, and help us to accomplish our goals. It's the irrational beliefs that get us in trouble and create the feelings of depression. What do you think about the belief, "I'm a failure." Rational or irrational?

R: Well, it sure doesn't help me, so I'd say irrational.

EN: Right. Beliefs that block us from achieving happiness, keep us from being more effective, and are defeating to self, others, or relationships are clearly irrational. That leads us to the final little d, **debating**. If I want to hold onto beliefs, they may as well be the ones that are enhancing and rational. Rational beliefs, those that lead to appropriate negative and positive emotions, can be supported, are logical, and would stand up in a psychological court of law. Irrational beliefs, on the other hand, are just the opposite. Although we might think that our irrational beliefs are factual and based on truth, we'll find that they aren't. When put to the test, they just don't stand up at all. So, that's what the **debating** phase is all about - putting our irrational beliefs on trial in order to disprove them and, more importantly, to change them to rational beliefs.

R: Yeah, but when I feel depressed, I really do believe that I'm a worthless failure.

EN: I realize that you do, and that's the point in detecting whether your belief can be supported. If you can prove that your belief is based on truth and facts, terrific! Just keep believing the way you do. By the way, do you believe in Santa?

R: What?

IT'S NOT AS BAD AS IT SEEMS

EN: Do you believe in Santa Claus?

R: (Sounding perplexed) Of course not.

EN: Did you ever believe in Santa Claus?

R: Sure I did. When I was a child . . .

EN: So why don't you believe in him today?

R: (Laughs) Well, when I was about five, I hid downstairs. I wanted to see Santa, but what I saw was my mother and father putting my toys out.

EN: So, you then instantly changed your beliefs about Santa?

R: No, I remember it taking a while. When my parents saw me, they took some time and talked with me about the spirit of Santa Claus, Christmas, and all of that.

EN: You got new information, and it was used to gradually disprove your belief that a living, breathing Santa existed. Right?

R: Yeah, I guess so.

EN: That's exactly what we're going to do now. Instead of testing the belief that there is a Santa Claus, we want to test the belief that you're a failure, that you are somehow pond scum. You believe that, because you've had some problems with relationships and you've failed at some important things, you are a failure. I want you to put that belief on trial right now and prove it beyond a shadow of a doubt.

R: It seems pretty obvious to me. If I were a better person and more desirable, I'd get more dates. Since I don't, I must be a failure.

EN: So, since you don't get the dates you'd like to have, that makes you a failure?

R: Yes.

IT'S NOT AS BAD AS IT SEEMS

EN: Ruth, what's a failure?

R: What?

EN: What's a failure? I mean, if a human is a failure, what percentage a failure are they?

R: I don't think I understand.

EN: Think about a horse for a minute. What percentage of a horse is a horse?

R: Where did horses come from?

EN Humor me for a second. In order to be a horse, what percent-age of a horse is necessary?

R: One hundred percent, of course.

EN: Right. If the animal is not 100 percent horse, it's probably a donkey or a mule or some other hybrid animal. So, if you think of yourself as being a failure, then what percentage failure are you?

R: Wait a minute, it's not the same.

EN: Sure it is. If you label yourself as a failure then it means that you are somehow a total failure as a human being. So, I guess that means that you've never succeeded at anything, right?

R: No, you know that's not true. I've been successful in lots of things.

EN: But, you keep telling me that you're a failure because you sometimes don't have dates or fail at certain things.

R: But, I feel like a failure.

EN: Because you feel like a failure, doesn't make you a failure. We call that **Emotional Reasoning**. If I feel depressed, I

94

am a depressed person. You feel depressed because you continually accept the silly notion that you are a failure, 100 percent bad and unworthy. But, let's get back to the challenging. You've told me that you feel like a failure sometimes, but I'm still waiting for you to prove to me you are a failure. Who dressed you this morning?

R: I did, of course.

EN: Were your teeth brushed?

R: Yes.

EN: Who brushed them?

R: I did.

EN: So you didn't fail to dress yourself and brush your teeth. So if you succeeded in these areas, is it possible for you to be a total failure, completely without worth as a human being?

R: No.

EN: You don't sound very convinced.

R: Those things don't seem to count very much when I compare them to some of the areas in my life where I have failed. Are you saying that those things just don't matter?

EN: Not at all. What I'm suggesting is that you magnify the negative and minimize the positive, and that you jump to conclusions. For example, because you don't have a date, that triggers your "stinking thinking" that "I'm a failure," and you take one little piece of information and draw conclusions that don't fit with the evidence. What I'm suggesting is that if you want to believe that you are a failure and totally without value as a person, that's okay, provided that you can support that notion beyond a shadow of a doubt. So, once more, prove to me that you are a failure.

R: When you put it like that, I guess I can't prove it.

IT'S NOT AS BAD AS IT SEEMS

EN: You guess?

R: I can't prove it. I'm successful in many areas.

EN: Let me be even more forceful. Is it logical to believe that because I misspell a word once, that I will always misspell it?

R: No.

EN: If a basketball player misses a shot, will he or she always miss the shot?

R: No.

EN: So it is not logical to maintain that because I fail at certain things, I am therefore a failure. We humans want to jump from the evidence we're given to far-fetched conclusions, and that's what you're doing. I will always fail at things, but because I fail at things does not make me a failure as a person. I have worth not because of what I do or what I have, but just because I exist. I have weaknesses and failings, but until there is a panel of expert judges on this earth who have 100 percent wisdom and can determine that some among us are 100 percent failures, then I choose to accept myself unconditionally as fallible human with the incurable tendency to make mistakes.

In Chapter Four, we talked about the three ways to dispute irrational beliefs - logical, empirical, and pragmatic. I am using a **logical disputation** with Ruth at this point. We too often just accept that our irrational thinking is in fact logical. I mean, after all, if we believe something, isn't it just logical to think that it's truth? Because I want there to be a Santa Claus, is it logical to think there is one? Because I deeply want fairness and world peace, is it logical to think there is world peace?

In order to change our irrational thinking, we begin testing the logic, reason, and sense of what we believe. The disputation question to ask is, "Is my belief reasonable, logical, and sensible?"

Does Ruth's logic make sense that because she may (and will!) fail at certain things, she is a failure as a person? Is it sensible to believe that because she may not always get the date she wants, she's a failure and will never have the dates she wants? The logic in these examples just doesn't hold water.

I'll want to help Ruth apply the logical disputation technique in many different situations so that she stops and asks herself, "Is this belief logical?" Is it logical to think that just because I feel like a failure sometimes that I am a failure? Is it logical to think that because I want a new car, I will suddenly have one? I wish that all of us thought logically, but we don't, and that is one of the goals of the thinking straight approach - to start thinking more logically especially as it relates to our personal problems.

R: So, you're saying that my logic is a little off when I start thinking of myself as a failure just because I may fail at things and not always have what I want?

EN: Yep, that's what I'm saying. To label yourself as a failure just because of failings is no more logical than for me to think I can beat a tennis pro in a game of tennis just because I take one lesson. Or, that I will get an "A" in a course just because I get an "A" on one homework assignment. Or, that it will be sunny tomorrow just because it's sunny today and was yesterday. If our beliefs about ourselves, others, or life conditions aren't logical, then it's in our best interest to change these to beliefs that are logical. What's a rational alternative, a more logical belief, to your belief that you're a failure?

R: I am not a failure?

EN: Is that a question or a statement?

R: A statement. I am not a failure.

EN: Remember Sgt. Carter on "Gomer Pyle, USMC," when he used to say, "I can't hear you!"

R: Yes.

EN: Well, Ruth, I can't hear you!

R: (More forcefully) I am **NOT A FAILURE.** Being human means I'm imperfect and I will fail at things, but I can never be a failure as a human being.

EN: Now let's test that belief to see if it is logical. You're telling me that you will in fact fail at things, but that won't make you a failure. Is that belief reasonable? Is it logical and sensible?

R: Sure, when I was in school, I rarely made 100 percent on the tests that I took, but I also rarely missed all the questions on the tests. If I failed on one of the questions, it meant just that. I missed a question. I wouldn't fail the test just because I missed one question. I really do see what you're saying. In some ways, I'm like one of those tests I took in school. I'll make mistakes, but I can never be a mistake as a person. I'll fail at certain things, and that won't make me a failure.

EN: What are you feeling right now?

R: Gee, this is interesting. I don't feel nearly as depressed as I did a few minutes ago.

EN: And why not?

R: I'm starting to change my thinking.

EN: You sure are. I'd like for you to get some more practice before this session is over. I want to teach you to use a variation of REI or **Rational-Emotive Imagery.**[5] Close your eyes, and in your mind's eye, picture last Saturday night. Get as vivid a mental picture as you can. Picture the room, what you are wearing, and as many details as possible. Let me know when you start to get the vivid image.

R: (After a brief pause) I've got the picture in my head.

EN: Good. Now as you imagine the scene, I want you to let yourself feel the same level of depression you felt that night. Really get in touch with the "9" intensity of depression. Take some time until you're really feeling the same emotional consequence you felt that night.

R: (Pause) Gosh, it's not hard at all. I can really feel the depression that I felt that Saturday night.

EN: That's great. Now notice what's going through your mind and what you're telling yourself. Identify those irrational beliefs we've been talking about. (Pauses) Now, I want you to change the depression to only disappointment. Push yourself to reduce the feeling from a "9" to only a "3" or "4." This is disappointment instead of depression. Let me know when you've done that.

R: (After about two or three minutes) Okay, I've got it. (Sounding excited.) I feel sad and disappointed, but not depressed. (She opens her eyes.)

EN: Fantastic! How did you do it? How did your thinking change?

R: When you had me recreate the scene and feel depressed, I just kept telling myself what a loser I was, and how being alone made me less of a·person. I kept pushing that non-sense through my head that because I'm alone on Saturday night, I'm a failure. I kept thinking that I'd always be alone. When you said to change the depression to disappointment, I really started testing out the logic of those statements. I asked myself if it was logical to think that because I was alone that I watherefore a loser or a failure. The answer was a loud and forceful **NO**. When I couldn't find any logic to support the thinking, then I started changing it to a belief that is logical, and like you said, would hold water. I started pushing the thought through my head that being alone on Saturday said absolutely nothing about my value as a human being. I kept thinking that being alone is a temporary condition, a situation, not a reflection of worth. I kept thinking I'm a person who is alone, not a lonely person who will always be lonely. I also told myself that I failed to have a

date tonight, but failing to have a date doesn't make me a
failure. As I started eliminating my irrational, illogical
beliefs with more rational, logical beliefs I noticed a distinct
change in how I was feeling.

EN: Ruth, you're doing a great job. What do you think would
happen if you practiced REI ten times each day?

R: I would think that it would get easier to change my irrational
beliefs to rational ones.

EN: You're right. So, in addition to your usual weekly homework of listening to the tape of this session, continuing to
read the therapy material, writing in your therapy journal,
and keeping your Daily Mood Log, I want you to practice
Rational-Emotive Imagery at least ten times each day. Each
time you practice, my bet is that you will have an easier and
easier time of changing the depressed feelings to feelings of
strong disappointment. Any questions or reactions to
today's session?

R: No. This was helpful.

EN: One more thing. Would you be willing to make a contract
with yourself and with me regarding your homework?

R: A contract? What type of contract?

EN: Well, we humans sometimes have a difficult time following
through. Sleeping, watching TV, and other distractions suddenly have more value than doing boring therapy homework
assignments. I like to use what is called **contingency
management** or creating a behavioral contract in order to
increase the likelihood that you will do your homework. It's
a contract that includes rewards and punishments. Would
you do it?

R: I'm serious about changing, so if it will help, sure.

EN: Excellent. What kinds of things do your really like to do?
Something that is a reward for you?

IT'S NOT AS BAD AS IT SEEMS

R: I kind of hate to admit it, but there are television shows, soap operas that are on at night, that I really like to watch.

EN: Okay. And what are some things that you really hate to do?

R: I hate to clean my bathrooms.

EN: If you spend 30 minutes every other day doing your therapy homework and practice your REI every day at least ten times, then you let yourself watch those favorite TV shows.

R: Sounds fair enough.

EN: And, if you don't complete the homework, then each day you haven't done the homework you spend 15 to 30 minutes cleaning your bathrooms.

R: Suddenly I feel very motivated to do the home-work!

EN: Good, then I'll see you next week.

Ruth accomplished a great deal during this second session. She learned more about the ABC's of thinking straight, gained a greater appreciation of the B-C Connection, and learned more about specific ways of disputing irrational beliefs, especially using logical types of disputes.

She learned about Rational-Emotive Imagery, which she can use daily to practice reducing her irrational thinking and inappropriate negative emotions like depression. She agreed to use some specific rewards and punishments, and by using this technique, she'll more likely complete her homework.

I routinely audiotape therapy sessions if clients agree, and since Ruth was taping her sessions, one of her homework assignments was to listen to the session in order to review the topics covered.

Before we take part in another therapy session with Ruth, I want you to think about other ways to dispute irrational beliefs. We reviewed logical types of disputes, but what are some other ways of disputing? Putting your therapist cap on, how would you have helped Ruth to dispute her irrational beliefs such as her belief that she is a failure? Review Chapter Four and write down your ideas below.

Ruth Backslides - The Sixth Session

Ruth has been making good progress in therapy. She actively completes the homework that she is given, and her Daily Mood Record has been reflecting a big change in her levels of depression. In recent weeks, her depression has averaged around a 5, and there are many days when she reports only feeling a 3 level of disappointment or sadness rather than depression.

She's been getting out a lot more and even having a number of dates. On weekends when she doesn't have a date, she is alert to the depression sharks that might get out of their cages. She has begun to enjoy these "dateless" weekends, though she would prefer, but not command or demand, to have a date.

Let's see how she's doing as we listen in on the sixth session.

R: I'm back at square one!

EN: What do you mean?

R: I thought I was doing so well, but obviously I wasn't. Last week was the pits. I felt great after our last session, and for the two days after that session. I had big plans for the weekend including a date with a guy I've been out with several times in the last month. I was psyched. Then on Thursday he calls me to tell me that "something had come up" and he was canceling our date. That was the beginning of the end! I was right back where I started from.

Attention therapists! Positions, everyone! What's going on with Ruth? Listen to her words and language: "beginning of the end," and "right back where I'd started from." Do you buy those statements? With the progress that Ruth's been making, would it be possible for her to be "back at square one?" As we continue, be thinking about what might be happening.

EN: The date got canceled, and what were you feeling?

R: Depressed. At first, I was just mildly depressed, about a "6" or so. But as time went on, I started feeling more and more depressed until by Sunday afternoon, I was back at "9" on the depression scale. I worked hard to figure out how come I was feeling so depressed, but no matter how hard I tried, I couldn't shake it.

EN: If you were in New York, San Francisco, Miami, Memphis, or some other large city, you had money, and you wanted to get to someplace that was too far to walk, how would you get there?

R: I'd probably take a cab.

EN: Right. And when you were stuck on Sunday, you could have done the same thing - taken a **CAB**.

R: What are you talking about?

EN: How do you spell cab?

R: C - A - B.

EN: Right. In RET, what does CAB stand for?

IT'S NOT AS BAD AS IT SEEMS

R: Oh, Consequences, Activators, and Beliefs.

EN: Correct. So you were stuck in deep waters with lots of irrational belief sharks swimming around. You felt depressed, but it sounds like you just stood there, or tread water there, with the sharks swimming about you.

R: I guess I did. No, I don't guess, I did!

EN: Anytime you feel stuck and want to work on the problem emotions and behaviors, take the RET CAB. Let's take the CAB now. What was the emotional consequence?

R: Depression that was at a "9" level of intensity.

EN: And the behavioral consequence?

R: The old avoidance techniques. I just sat at home feeling depressed and sorry for myself. Wouldn't get out of the house.

EN: And the activator?

R: Well, I'm not sure about that. At first, it was the guy calling off the date. But I think I dealt pretty well with that. I felt a little depressed, but even after I told myself that it wasn't the end of the world that the date was called off, I kept getting more and more depressed.

EN: When you felt the initial mild depression, did you have any particular thoughts?

R: Yes, as a matter of fact I did. When I got off the phone, I rated my gut feelings and recognized that I was feeling some depression. I was telling myself that I could stand not having a date that weekend, but I kept thinking that I shouldn't feel depressed about it.

EN: Oh, I see. So you started "shoulding on" yourself because you were feeling what you were feeling, even though you didn't want to feel that way.

IT'S NOT AS BAD AS IT SEEMS

R: I guess I did.

EN: It seems to me that the Activator wasn't the date being called off but rather the fact that you were feeling mildly depressed about the disappointment. In RET, there is something that we call **symptom stress**. This is when emotional consequences becomes the activator. In your case, the date was called off, the activator, and you felt mildly depressed about that, so the depression was the emotional consequence. Then the mild depression moved from point C to point A and became an activator. You were feeling depressed but then you started having specific irrational beliefs about the depression, thoughts such as, "I shouldn't feel this way." Right?

R: Exactly. I've been in therapy now for almost two months and have had five sessions. I've read the pamphlets and other material you suggested, have been doing my homework, and all the other stuff. And yet, with all of that, here I am feeling depressed. I've failed again!

EN: You've had only five sessions, you've been doing a terrific job, and you're making excellent progress. We've talked about the likelihood that you'll attend probably 12 to 24 therapy sessions spread out over nine to 18 months. After only five sessions, you feel mildly depressed, and that triggers the self-damning shark . . . .

R: (Interrupts) But, I shouldn't feel depressed!

ER: Where is that written?

R: What?

EN: EN: Where is it written that after five therapy sessions Ruth **SHOULD NOT, MUST NOT** feel mildly depressed from time to time? Did the hot line from God ring? Did He tell you there was a missing commandment that says, "Ruth shalt not feel depressed after five therapy sessions."

R: You're making fun of me!

105

EN: No, I'm not making fun of you, but I am encouraging you to make fun of that belief, that you shouldn't feel depressed from time to time. Remember you're taking a RET CAB right now, and I think you've found the irrational belief that resulted in your feeling increasingly depressed. What do you think?

R: I agree. I was shoulding on myself and putting myself down. I was feeding myself a bunch of irrational crap.

EN: So, you've identified the irrational belief shark that resulted in your feeling increasingly depressed. You were damning yourself and shoulding on yourself with that belief. You're pretty good at using logical types of disputation, so how about applying an empirical disputation technique with this belief?

R: You mean like, "Where's the evidence that would prove that I shouldn't be feeling what I was feeling?"

EN: Exactly. Where is the evidence that would support the belief that at that moment in time you must not have been feeling mildly depressed?

R: It's not written anywhere that I know of.

EN: Me either. Is there a new law of the universe, a new law of physics that says Ruth **MUST** never feel mildly depressed?

R: I don't think so, but what do you mean?

EN: There is a law of physics that says if I drop my pen, it will always fall as long as it is in our atmosphere. But, over the weekend, it was like you wanted to create a new law of the universe that says, "Ruth must never feel depressed." Let me ask you since in this situation you really are the expert, did you feel depressed?

R: Yes.

EN: So, factually, realistically, and empirically, there is no universal law or law of physics that says you must not, should not feel depressed because in fact you did feel that way. If there was such an universal law that says you or anybody shouldn't feel depressed after five therapy sessions, then guess what? After five sessions, people would never get depressed again. It would be physically impossible, just like it would be physically impossible for the pen to float naturally in our atmosphere. There is no physical evidence.or fact--ual support for the belief that you must not ever feel depressed, mildly or otherwise. What's a rational alternative?

R: I very much wish that I hadn't felt depressed, but I did. I'm not immune from depression or other feelings. In fact, as a human, I will feel many different feelings. I certainly would have preferred strongly that I not have felt even mildly depressed, but again, realistically speaking, I did. Because I felt depressed simply meant that I was given an opportunity to practice my RET skills, and at worst, I failed to effectively use the skills in that situation. But, failing in that situation didn't make me a failure.

EN: Great! Since, in the psychological court of law, you can't support the irrational belief, "I shouldn't feel depressed," you've chosen to replace that non-supportable belief with the rational alternative at point **E**, the effects of disputing, or the new effective philosophy. The new belief is, "I feel depressed. I wish I didn't feel depressed, but I do, and it in no way makes me a failure. Depression is extremely uncomfortable, but I have the skills necessary in order to change depression into disappointment or sadness."

Ruth, what if you'd be feeling so depressed that you couldn't or wouldn't be able to apply the empirical or logical forms of disputation? How else might you have been able to dispute your self-downing related to feeling depressed?

R: You mean using practical disputation or coping self-statements?

EN: Yes, tell me how you could have done that.

R: If I remember correctly, a practical or pragmatic type of disputing involves asking myself how it is helping to be feeling and thinking the way I am at that moment. For example, if I had taken the RET CAB and determined that I was shoulding on myself for feeling depressed, I could have asked myself, "Ruth, how is it helping you right now to keep telling yourself that you shouldn't be feeling what in fact you are feeling?" Or I could have asked how it was helping to keep telling myself that I was a failure for feeling mildly depressed. I could have asked myself if feeling depressed and upsetting myself was helping in any positive way. I've found that if I ask myself if thinking a particular way helps or hurts, then I get some good information about whether I'm thinking rationally or irrationally. Are those examples?

EN: Those are great examples. For me, if my empirical and logical debates haven't been successful, then I can always, or at least almost always, count on practical disputes. What about using a coping self-statement?

R: You mean like, "I don't like it, that's okay, I can stand it anyway!" Something like that?

EN: That's one example, what about some others?

R: Sometimes when I feel depressed, I remind myself that depression is an emotion or an emotional consequence and not a permanent condition. I tell myself that because I feel depressed today, it in no way means that I will feel depressed tomorrow or next week. I also forcefully tell myself that I'm doing a pretty terrific job in therapy and that I'm making progress, and that it is natural and expected to feel some degree of depression from time to time. I remind myself of that thing you taught me, the **FEELS** example you said you heard somebody use once.[6] If I feel depressed, or any other emotion for that matter, I first **FACE IT**. Then I remind myself to **EXPECT IT**. That is, to remember that I will feel all kinds of different feelings and that is natural. Then, my task is to fully **EXPERIENCE IT**. Like you've said so many times, feelings are not necessarily enemies and can be allies or signals from which we can learn. I let myself notice where in my body I'm feeling what I'm feeling so I can use that as a clue in the future. With this information, I

108

can **LEARN FROM THE FEELING.** Then I can begin to **LET IT GO,** by **MAKING RATIONAL STATE-MENTS TO MYSELF.** You know, by the time I get to that point, whatever it is that I'm feeling doesn't seem so bad anymore.

EN: Boy, Ruth, you are learning a lot. What are you feeling now?

R: Only a little disappointed that I didn't use my skills as well as I would have liked to. But, I realize I feel better than when I felt depressed and that meant that my shark had gotten out. I am seeing that it was only too bad that I didn't practice my skills perhaps as well as I could have, and not that I was a failure. Thinking rationally is getting more and more automatic, and it is easier to apply the thinking straight skills.

With a client like Ruth, therapy would probably continue over several months. I usually like to increase the time between sessions after I believe that the client has developed a good set of thinking straight skills. Application of the skills in the world outside of therapy is "proof of the rational thinking pudding."

I want clients to be able to apply many different types of disputation techniques and not rely on just one or two types of disputing. I also emphasize that chances are all of us will backslide at some time. That is one reason I give clients a copy of the pamphlet *How to Maintain and Enhance Your Rational-Emotive Therapy Gains,* by Dr. Ellis.[7] To help reduce the chances of serious backsliding, I often schedule a booster session in four to twelve weeks.

Suggested Homework for Chapter Six:

I want you to have a booster session right now and to take the RET CAB. Think on an example from the last week or two when you felt inappropriately depressed, angry, anxious, or frus-

trated. Now use the space below to outline the emotional and behavioral consequences, the activator, and your specific beliefs about
the activator.

Now, use as many different disputation techniques as you
can come up with to attack the sharks and get them back in the
cages. Use a combination of empirical, logical, and practical disputes. Remember to measure the intensity of the feelings as a way
of seeing your success. You may also want to use some of the techniques used with Ruth in this chapter such as Rational-Emotive Imagery. Take time right now and practice the skills. Best of success!

CHAPTER SEVEN

"We Never Talk Anymore":
Working on Relationship Problems

In the last chapter, we learned about Ruth and the problems she had with depression. I have talked a lot about problems that individuals have, but many individuals are also involved in important loving or liking relationships. When individuals get together in "we" relationships, some problems are sure to erupt, some big and some small.

In this chapter, you will meet Carol and Ted and see how their "stinking thinking" (especially irrational thinking that creates anger and frustration) was a big part of their marital problems. Since this chapter will give only a brief introduction to some of the problems couples experience, I would like to mention some books based on the "thinking straight" approach to change that I have found helpful over the years.

Two books that I almost always recommend to people with relationship problems are *Love Is Never Enough*[1] by Dr. Aaron Beck, and *The Three Faces of Love*[2] by Dr. Paul Hauck. Other books written by Dr. Ellis that have helped many people deal with relationship problems include *A New Guide to Rational Living*[3] and *How to Live with a Neurotic.*[4]

Meet Carol and Ted

Carol and Ted were in their mid-thirties and had been married for eight years. They had one child, Stacia, age five. Carol was a nurse and Ted worked as an accountant for a small firm.

IT'S NOT AS BAD AS IT SEEMS

They had met at a party and dated for about three years before they decided to marry.

They both agreed that the first four years of marriage had been "blissful" and that they had rarely argued. When asked what attracted them to each other, Ted described Carol as being "fun-loving" and spontaneous, and Carol said she liked Ted's ability to "think things through," his sensitivity, and his ability to manage money well.

The first several sessions had focused on identifying the specific problems that got in the way of their having the type of loving relationship they each said they wanted. Some of the problems were vague, like Carol's complaint that she "didn't feel loved," and Ted's similar complaint of, "I don't feel Carol appreciates me." Other problems were much more concrete, such as "We fight rather than discuss problems," and "We never talk." Both complained of feeling very angry and frustrated.

The Rational-Emotive Therapy "thinking straight" approach to relationship problems is similar to the approach taken when addressing individual problems. It involves making both cognitive (thought) and behavioral (action) changes.

The first step involved defining and agreeing on the problems and goals to be worked on in therapy. Carol and Ted agreed that their goals were to improve their communication, reduce the number of arguments they had, reduce the feelings of anger and frustration, and increase the specific actions and behaviors that would result in their feeling more loved and appreciated. They were introduced to the ABC's of Rational-Emotive Therapy and taught the B-C (Belief-Consequence) Connection.

This is the third psychotherapy session with Carol and Ted. Let's listen in and see how it's going.

EN: How did last week go?

C: To tell you the truth, I was actually kind of surprised. Surprised because the week went so well. I don't know what it was, but maybe we were paying more attention to each other and trying harder.

T: I'd agree with that. Or, at least it went well for the first part of the week. Then Carol's anger reared its ugly head. Kind of like a monster just lurking in the background waiting to come out and mess up the week that was going well. I really think that one of the biggest problems in our relationship is Carol's anger. If she'd just change and learn how to control anger, I think everything would be fine. I really think she needs to work on that during today's session.

When couples finally decide to start therapy, often they are almost certain that if the other person would just change, everything would be just fine! Both Carol and Ted suffer from the "It's thee, not me" syndrome. Ted has just attempted to put the responsibility of the relationship problems on to Carol.

In individual and couple's therapy, I strongly emphasize that each person is responsible for his or her own thinking, feeling, and behavior, and that each person can either be part of the problem or part of the solution. I am not going to be willing to accept Ted's definition of the problem (that is, Carol's anger), but I will attempt to help Ted take ownership of his role in the conflict.

EN: Ted, I don't know if Carol's anger is a big part of the problem or not. But, just for a minute, let's accept that she does have a problem with anger. When she gets angry, how do you react?

T: When she gets angry, that really makes me mad!

Magical Thinking

Time for you to put that trusty therapist hat on again. Ted is saying Carol's anger makes him mad. What do you think of that?

IT'S NOT AS BAD AS IT SEEMS

Is it a true statement? Write down what you would say to Ted.

I'll bet you would point out to Ted that the statement that Carol's anger makes him angry suggests that she has some type of magical power over Ted. I call it "**magical thinking**" because it is an A-C (Activator-Consequence) Connection, which would mean that other people's emotions, like anger, control our feelings and "make us" feel other particular emotions.

I would also guess that you would then point out to Ted that while Carol's anger may indeed contribute to and influence his feelings, it is his beliefs about it that determine how he feels and what he does, not her feelings alone. Let's see what I do.

EN: Does her anger make you angry?

T: Sure.

EN: So, when she's angry, it's like she points an emotional ray gun at you, pulls the trigger, and forces you to feel anger. If it's true that she makes you angry, then I guess you have no control over your emotions. Is that true?

C: Yeah, I don't make him mad, but this is typical of Ted. Always blaming me for everything!

EN: Carol, you're saying that you don't want Ted to get angry just because you're feeling anger at the moment?

C: Yes. Ted's a big boy, and just because I may be feeling angry, it doesn't mean that he has to get himself all worked up.

EN: Let me ask you both. Who *is* responsible for our feelings,
based on what we have talked about in earlier sessions and the
reading that you have been doing?

T: I know you keep saying over and over again that we are responsible for our own thinking, feeling, and behavior, and
that we are responsible to each other as adults but not for the
other's thinking, feeling, and behavior.

EN: But?

T: But, that sounds good. But, all I know is, every time Carol
gets angry, I end up getting angry, too.

C: And when Ted gets angry because I'm angry, then I usually
end up getting even angrier.

EN: I certainly agree with you both that anger in your relationship
is a big part of the problem. Anger gets in the way of caring
behaviors, effective communication, and good problem-
solving skills. Ted, if Carol had some rare disease that literally controlled her emotions and in fact would cause her to get
angry with you for no good reason, do you think you would
get as angry as you do now every time she got angry?

T: I doubt it.

EN: Why not?

T: I guess because there would be a reason for her anger.

EN: But, there is a reason for her anger now!

C: Yeah, because he doesn't do what I want!

EN: Carol, let me stick with Ted for right now. Ted, if Carol had a
disorder that somehow resulted in her feeling angry, you
wouldn't make yourself as angry about her anger. The

difference would be your *thinking* about her anger. When she gets angry now, what goes through your mind?

T: She's always getting angry at me, and she should not react that way! If she loves me, she shouldn't get so mad at me!

EN: And what if she had that rare imaginary anger disease, and she got angry. What would you say to yourself?

T: Her disease is flaring up again, and that's just the way it is. I can't control her anger, and neither can she. I don't like it but I can stand it.

EN: And how are the two belief systems different?

T: I'm not sure.

EN: Carol, how about you? How are the two ways of thinking different?

C: When I'm angry and Ted gets angry, it's like he's demanding that I not be feeling angry. It's like he's "shoulding on" me for being angry. And he seems to personalize it, you know, like when I get angry, I'm doing it to him.

EN: Ted, is that accurate?

T: Yes, but she shouldn't get so angry at me for no good reason!

EN: When was that law passed?

T: What?

EN: You remember we've talked about when humans play God and write laws and rules in their heads, as if they were the laws of the universe?

T: Yeah.

EN: Well, it sounds like you've written one of those laws. It reads, Carol **MUST** not, **SHOULD** not get angry with me

116

for no good reason. But Ted, does she ever get angry with you for no good reason?

Time to Dispute

I am beginning to have Ted dispute his own underlying irrational belief. I am picking up on his tendency to musturbate, that is, to demand and command Carol not get angry at him. But she does!

In earlier chapters we talked about empirical, logical, and practical (or pragmatic) ways of disputing irrational beliefs. What type of disputation have I just used?

If you said empirical, you're right. Factually, Carol does get angry with Ted, whether for good or bad reasons. His anger is caused not by her anger but rather by his internal (and external) demands that she *must* not be feeling what she is in fact feeling at that moment in time.

If there was a universal law that said spouses **MUST, OUGHT, SHOULD** never feel angry with their partners, then guess what? They wouldn't! But reality is that people feel anger and show it in different ways, no matter how much others may dislike it or object to it.

Musturbation is almost always at the root of anger problems, and when I'm doing couple's therapy, anger is frequently a major issue.

Now I want to help Ted reduce his anger by helping him to empirically dispute the demand that he has written.

T: Yeah, she gets mad a lot.

EN: But, if there were a law of the universe that said Carol SHOULD NOT, MUST NOT ever get angry, then she would not, because it would be a supportable, natural law,

117

like the law of gravity. So where is the evidence that supports your belief that Carol must not get angry with you?

T: If you look at it that way, there is no evidence. But I don't like it!

EN: Sure, and that makes sense. You don't like it when she feels anger and it is directed at you. But, just because you don't like it doesn't mean that she shouldn't feel it. And is it logical for you to maintain the belief that just because you don't like something, like Carol's anger, then it **must** not exist?

Following the empirical disputation, I am introducing the logical type of dispute. Not only is there no hard evidence to support Ted's notion that because he doesn't like his wife's anger, she must not get angry, but also, there is no logic. It is "magical thinking" for me to believe that if I find something unpleasant, it should not exist.

Asking Ted to look at the practical consequences of his holding on to his irrational demands illustrates the practical or pragmatic type of disputing underlying irrational beliefs. As with the empirical and logical disputes, he is better able to see that his demands that his wife not feel what she feels and that she be the way he wants her to be are clearly irrational, defeating to himself and to the relationship.

Anger does beget anger in most situations, and as Ted learns to manage his angry feelings in a more constructive fashion, it is likely to help reduce the overall anger problem in the relationship.

Ted, you've just done a great job of disputing the belief that Carol should not get angry with you for no good reason. Now, have you come up with any support for this belief?

T: No.

EN: So, if you can't prove the belief, where does that leave you? What would you suggest doing at this point?

T: Since I don't and can't control Carol's feelings of anger, or her other feelings for that matter, and since I can't support my belief that she shouldn't feel what she feels, it would probably be a good idea for me to change my thinking.

EN: Super! But change your thinking how?

T: I could change an irrational belief to a rational alternative.

EN: And what might that be?

T: Change the commandment or demand to a verifiable, supportable, enhancing belief. I really don't like it when she gets mad at me, and I really do strongly wish that she would work on feeling less anger toward me and expressing her anger in a more constructive fashion when she does feel anger. But, I can want and wish for it all day long, and that doesn't mean she has to change. That's it. I can change the demand to a want.

EN: Yes, and she may still be angry at you. And how will you feel if you change your irrational demand to a rational preference, and she's still angry with you for no good reason?

T: I'll still feel strongly annoyed. But, I know myself well enough to know that if I'm only irritated, I probably won't blow up at Carol and become part of the problem.

As you read this section of the therapy session, it may well sound like I'm doing individual therapy with Ted. In many ways, I am, and I will frequently spend time with one partner working on his or her specific underlying irrational beliefs.

I believe it is preferable to do this work while the other partner is in the therapy room. In many ways, it helps the other partner learn more about the person who is working. It is much more cost-effective than spending time with each partner separately in individual therapy. It also serves to model for the partner who is listening how to go about identifying the A, B, C, D, E, and F of Rational-Emotive Therapy. That's what I'm going to do now with Carol.

EN: Carol, I want you to be the supervising therapist now. Put what Ted's been working on into the ABC framework of RET. What was the emotional C that Ted identified?

C: You mean the consequences?

EN: Yes.

C: The emotion that he identified was anger.

EN: And was the anger appropriate or inappropriate?

C: I'd say inappropriate, because as he said, when he gets angry in response to my anger, it only pours fuel on the fire.

EN: I agree. And what was the A, the activator?

C: Sounds like my anger served to activate his anger.

EN: And what about the B, or belief? What were the beliefs that Ted had that created his anger in response to your anger?

C: Was it musturbation?

EN: What do you think?

C: I think it was. I picked up on his demand that I *must* not feel angry with him. It was the "playing God syndrome" of insisting that what was should not be.

EN: And what happened then?

C: You moved from C to D, to disputing the underlying irrational beliefs once they were detected. I've been having a problem with debating and disputing irrational beliefs, and I was listening while you were helping Ted dispute his beliefs. Would you review the specific types of questions that can be used to dispute irrational beliefs?

EN: Sure. If I'm choosing to believe any particular belief, I'll want to ask myself for the evidence that supports the belief. So one important question is, "Where's the evidence for the belief, other than in my head?" Asking yourself to "Prove it" is another important way of debating. In other words, can I prove the belief beyond a shadow of a doubt? I know that the belief may seem real, but I'm looking for scientific facts to support it, not just feelings or hunches.

Another question to use during disputing is to ask whether the belief is logical or not. I may think that people shouldn't get angry at me, but is there any logic in believing that what is shouldn't be? Is it logical to believe that because I don't like something, it must change?

And finally, another question to ask yourself during the disputation process is, "How is my believing that Carol should not be angry with me going to help reduce the anger in our relationship?" Be creative when disputing irrational beliefs. Try out different techniques and styles of disputing.

So, once you've disputed the underlying irrational belief, then what?

C: From D you go to E, the effects of disputing. Ted pointed out that after disputing his irrational belief, he was able to change the demand, the must and the should, to a preference. He still didn't like the fact that I was reacting angrily toward him, but he changed the absolutistic belief to a strong preference. He was able to create a rational alternative, which was that he wishes I wouldn't react the way I did, but I did. He had no control over my thinking and feeling, but he did have control over his own thinking. I heard him change the "She shouldn't" to "I wish she wouldn't."

EN: And what happened at point F, or the new feelings?

C: Anger changed to only irritation and annoyance. And it makes sense that if we are only feeling annoyed or irritated, then we will be better able to communicate more effectively and solve problems.

IT'S NOT AS BAD AS IT SEEMS

Can We Talk?

Carol's right. The title of this chapter is "We Never Talk Anymore" and you may have wondered what this part of therapy had to do with effective communication. Have you ever tried to talk to someone when you were really angry? What happened?

For me, anger and effective communication tend to be mutually exclusive. Anger serves to "shut down" my ability to reason and to express myself in a clear and appropriate way. When I'm busy "shoulding on" people around me, I am more interested in proving my point and being right than I am in give-and-take communication. I am not interested in understanding what the other person is saying, but only in "making" that person see my point and understand my position.

In loving relationships such a pattern is like a boxing match - trying to score points and knock the other person out. You may win the round and be "right," but you may also be "dead right" and lose the relationship. Many times people tend to wrap their "egos" and "self-worth" up in the package of being right and proving their partners or others wrong. We tend to think "win-lose" rather than "win-win." "If I don't prove my point, then I'll lose!" "If I don't stand my ground, my partner will walk all over me!"

What would happen, in reality, if you did give a little? What if you said to your friend, spouse, parent, child, or co-worker, "You know, I hadn't looked at it that way, maybe you're onto something." Such a different response is available when the requiring philosophy is changed to a desiring philosophy. We stop dogmatically insisting that others see it our way, and allow for individual differences. If we are practicing unconditional self-acceptance, then we know that our worth as a person is not tied to getting others to see it our way.

Before we continue to work with Carol and Ted, I want you to stop and think about your own important relationships. If you are currently involved in a significant loving relationship, whether a dating, marital, or family relationship, I want you to bring the "magical" video camera out of storage. This is the camera that picks up on thoughts and feelings, and can offer us insight into our own "stinking thinking" and defeating behaviors.

122

IT'S NOT AS BAD AS IT SEEMS

As you play back a tape of you relating to important people in your life, what are some of the underlying irrational beliefs that might be interfering with these relationships? Do you share anything in common with Carol and Ted and their tendency to demand that the other see things a certain way?

Take a personal inventory in order to uncover any patterns of thinking, feeling, and acting that may be part of a problem rather than being part of a solution. Below write down what you come up with, and then use the ABC format to attack the underlying sharks of irrational thinking.

Now that you have taken the time to think about some of your irrational thinking sharks that may interfere with your relationships, let's see what's happening with Carol and Ted.

C   I do see how my anger is certainly part of the problem, and I'm willing to work on this. But one of the things that I really find upsetting is my feeling that Ted just doesn't love me.

EN: What do you think about that, Ted? Carol gets the idea that you don't love her. Do you?

T: Sure I do. I wouldn't be here right now if I didn't. I really can't believe that she's saying that. Think about it, Carol. Didn't I just buy you that new refrigerator that you wanted?

C: A refrigerator is nice, and I did want it, but buying me a refrigerator doesn't help me to feel loved. I would much rather you spend less time at the office and more time at home.

When I work in relationship therapy, I tell couples that progressing in therapy will be like pouring the foundation for a house. The corners of that foundation will represent the different skills necessary for creating and maintaining a loving, mutually supportive relationship. These skills will include identifying specific irrational beliefs and inferences that create unhealthy emotions like anger and frustration, reinforcing particular behaviors and actions that will be used to communicate "I love you" with actions, and developing and sharpening overall communications skills, and in some cases, problem-solving skills, parenting skills, and other specific skills that may be necessary to improve the relationship.

As the old saying goes, "Actions speak louder than words." And when there are problems in a relationship, this is especially true. While teaching couples about the ABC's of emotional and relationship difficulties, it is also important to teach them how they can create consistency between the words, "I love you," and their accompanying behaviors.

Too often, each individual in the relationship will insist that he or she deeply loves the other and is profoundly committed to improving the relationship. But there is often a lack of harmony between the words that merely say, "I love you" and the actions and behaviors that often scream, "I don't care about you!"

Since talk is cheap (unless people are talking to therapists or attorneys!), I believe that it is important to measure commitment and love with action, not just talk.

Caring Behaviors

But, can love and commitment be measured? Can "I love you" be translated into specific actions?

I think the answer to both of these questions is "Yes." Several years ago, I was fortunate enough to attend a workshop on relationship therapy given by Drs. Richard B. Stuart and Barbara Jacobson. During this workshop, they presented a concept called "**Caring Behaviors**" that I have found very useful. It has become one of the corners of the foundation of healthy relationships that I present to couples.

Drs. Stuart and Jacobson have defined caring behaviors as "verbal or nonverbal expressions of interest, respect, concern, and/or affection that can be offered many times each week."[5]

Such frequent, small acts of love, affection, and caring create and maintain loving relationships and say with actions, "Hey, I'm really committed to our relationship." While "saying it with flowers" may be one way to demonstrate love, "saying it with caring behaviors" is a method by which love can be translated into action and measured.

Drs. Stuart and Jacobson offer some tips on creating and using caring behaviors, or what I have come to call "**CBs.**" CB s are, for example:

1. Positive and specific actions and behaviors, rather than making a caring behavior something like, "Don't criticize me," a person might include, "Compliment me on how I look."

2. Actions that can be desired by either partner or both partners.

3. Actions or behaviors that can occur at least once a week.

4. Actions or behaviors that have not been the subject of major arguments in the past.

5. Any desired actions, regardless of whether they already occur regularly, have occurred, in the past but not recently, or have never occurred, as this is a completely new request.[6]

One of the assignments that Carol and Ted will be given at the end of this session will be to develop a caring behaviors list. Each will be asked to begin by defining five specific behaviors and actions that, once completed, would communicate love, appreciation, respect, and commitment.

As I mentioned at the beginning of this chapter, Rational-Emotive "thinking straight" therapy encourages people to change not only their irrational beliefs and attitudes, but also their self- and relationship-defeating behaviors. Caring behaviors are one way that people can show each other their commitment. Often, these changes in behavior also serve to influence changes in thinking.

Now I want to help Carol and Ted begin to specifically define some caring behaviors.

EN: Carol, if Ted could put love into actions, what are called caring behaviors, what kind of specific, small things could he do to show you with his behavior that he loves you?

C: I would really like it if he would tell me that he loves me, give me a hug from time to time, especially when he leaves the house and comes home, or watch a TV show with me every now and then. Sometimes my back and shoulders really hurt and it would be great if he would give me a massage. I'd also like it if he'd put Stacia to bed sometimes.

EN: That's a great start for a "Caring Days Inventory." I like how you've been very specific about what you're asking for from Ted, as caring behaviors can be completed often. Ted, how about you? What are some caring behaviors that you would like to receive from Carol?

T: I go for a walk every night when I get home from work and it would be nice if Carol would go with me. One of my hobbies is music, and it would mean a lot to me if she would listen to music with me. Some other caring behaviors would be to go to church with me, ask me how my day was, and spend time just talking with me.

I reviewed with Carol and Ted the concept of caring behaviors, and gave them the homework assignment to write a list of five to ten "CB's" for each of them.

The caring behaviors list was to be taped to the bathroom mirror, since they both agreed they would be more likely to see it and review it each morning. During the day, they would demonstrate several of the caring behaviors on the list, and when the CB's were received, each would acknowledge the other's caring actions in two ways, by saying so with words and by putting the date the caring behavior was offered on the **"Caring Days Inventory"**[7] they were using. At the end of each day, they would spend time reviewing the inventory, just in case some of the caring behaviors were overlooked.

The Five-Minute Date - The Eighth Session

Even though Carol and Ted said that the first four years of marriage were "blissful," as therapy has progressed there has been evidence that their sharks of anger and frustration have been swimming in their waters for a long time.

Because of these deeply ingrained irrational beliefs, therapy has moved at a slow pace. There have been ups and downs, and this is a natural part of the change process.

Both have been reluctant to complete homework assignments and have tended to wait for the other to initiate the homework. We have discussed the **"Change First Principle,"**[8] which says that each person is responsible for changing and practicing the new patterns of thinking, feeling, and acting, even if the other person does not do so. Nonetheless, the undercurrent seems to be "I'm not going to change unless he/she does!"

Standing homework assignments included engaging in caring behaviors each day, adding behaviors to the Caring Days Inventory, listening to the audio tape of the therapy session, and having a **"Five-Minute Date"** each day. The "five-minute date" involves setting aside five minutes of uninterrupted time to talk, to listen, and to review their progress.

As you will see, the past week had not gone well at all! The session started with a review of the homework. Let's join Carol and Ted.

EN: I'd like to review the homework, including the addition of new caring behaviors, the five-minute dates, and your impressions from review of the last therapy session tape.

C: (Angrily) Before we even get started, I think we better talk about whether this marriage even has a snowball's chance in hell of surviving! I've just about had it! Ted is more interested in staying at work and helping his clients than he is in being with his family. He's not doing any of the homework, and he's always waiting for me to start everything.

T: You've got lots of room to talk! All you do is complain and whine about all the things that I'm not doing! When was the last time you asked me how my day was?

Do you notice the pronoun that both Carol and Ted keep using? Both of them are focused on the other person's perceived shortcomings and failings. Carol keeps "taking Ted's inventory," and Ted keeps saying "you . . . you . . . you . . . " in referring to what Carol is and isn't doing.

One element of effective communication is ownership of thoughts, feelings, and actions. Ownership begins with "I" statements. "You" statements suggest that blame is being dumped onto the other person, and it's up to him or her to make the changes.

Let's see what I ask Carol and Ted to do with their communication pattern.

EN: How are both of you feeling right now?

T: Angry!

C: Yeah, me too. I'm real angry and frustrated.

EN: As you two are talking right now, I have the mental image in my head of both of you pointing your finger at the other. Would you humor me for a second and do that? Actually point your finger at each other and vigorously move your hands as if you're scolding each other.

T: I really don't want . . . .

EN: Just try it right now if you will.

IT'S NOT AS BAD AS IT SEEMS

[Both Carol and Ted point their fingers at each other.]

EN: What feelings go with that action?

C: I just keep feeling more and more angry.

EN: Ted, what about you?

T: Same, I feel about a 9 angry on the 10-point scale.

EN: And what's going through your head right now?

T: She's blaming me again, and she shouldn't do that! It's her fault, not mine!

C: I keep thinking, "How dare he blame me! I can't stand it when he does that!"

EN: What's serving to activate some of those thoughts and feelings?

C: He keeps blaming me.

EN: Even though you two don't literally wave your fingers in each others' faces, it seems to me that many times when you're talking with each other, you wave your fingers with words. I notice that the pronouns you, he, and she get used a lot, but I don't hear the pronoun "I" used nearly as often. I want you to learn both thinking and doing skills that will help improve your relationship. One of the doing skills has to do with effecive communication. One part of effective communication is ownership of thoughts, feelings, and actions. I wonder what would happen if instead of all the "you" pronouns, each of you worked on using "I" more. Carol, you perceive that Ted is not doing the therapy homework the way you'd like for him to do it and you seem to feel angry. Are there any other feelings besides anger that you have when he doesn't do the homework?

C: Yeah, hurt. When he doesn't spend time on the homework, it's like he doesn't care.

129

EN: Doesn't care about what?

C: Me, the relationship, or the family.

Active Listening

    In social psychology there is a concept called "Attribution Theory." Prejudice involves attribution theory because we attribute negative aspects and negative characteristics to groups or people about whom we often know very little. We attach negative meaning to a single action, characteristic, or statement, and then we over-generalize and jump to the conclusion that the person or group is bad, wicked, or just "no damn good."

    Prejudice is present in dating, living, loving, and marital relationships, too. We often develop a "mind set" about our beloved when we're dating, and "in lust," that he or she can do no wrong, that his or her behavior is "cute," or maybe he or she is "assertive."

    When conflict develops in the relationship, the positive prejudice many times becomes negative prejudice, and we begin to see the other person's behavior through brown-tinted glasses instead of rose-tinted glasses. With this prejudice in place, we attribute negative meaning to actions, statements, and behaviors.

    Ted's not doing the homework takes on special and very negative meaning for Carol. She attributes "he doesn't care" or "he doesn't love me" to his not completing assignments. Having drawn that conclusion, she then clears the way for the anger, frustration, and depression sharks to start getting out. Ted as well attributes negative meaning to Carol's behaviors and starts "shoulding on" her, based on his conclusions. Effective communication can help people to get to know each other better, which can serve to reduce prejudice and conflict in relationships.

EN: Ted, is that accurate? Does your not completing homework assignments mean you don't love Carol?

T: Of course not! I've just been so busy at work. After all, it is tax time!

EN: Let's back up for a minute. Let's pretend we've got a video of the last five-minute exchange. We want to edit it to reflect more effective communication and increase the probability that "message sent equals message heard."9 I'd like for both of you start over and use "I" statements. Rather than blaming the other, make statements that reflect what you are feeling and thinking, and also what you might want the other person to do differently which would be a caring behavior.

C: Ted, when you spend so much time at work and don't have time to do the homework or listen to the therapy session tapes, I feel hurt and angry.

EN: Good. And tell Ted what types of thoughts go through your mind about his not doing the homework.

C: I tell myself that because you don't take the time to do the homework, it means you don't care.

EN: Great. You're doing a nice job of directly and assertively expressing your thoughts and feelings. And now it's important to "check out" the accuracy of the meaning that you attach to his not doing the homework, that he doesn't care. So ask him if your impression is accurate?

C: Ted, is that accurate? When you don't do the homework, does it mean that you don't care?

T: No. I promise you it doesn't say anything about how much I love you and care about you. If anything, it reflects my poor time management, especially around this time of year.

EN: How do you feel right now, Ted, as Carol more directly expresses her feelings and thoughts?

T: I don't feel angry with Carol. I do feel disappointed that I don't manage my time better, but that's disappointment about my behavior, not Carol's.

EN: And Carol, what are you feeling and thinking?

C: When Ted clarifies and lets me know that he does love me, my anger also goes down because I'm not reading so much into his not being at home. He's provided an understandable reason for staying at work, and I'm not shoulding on him.

EN: Ted, I'd like for you to edit your part of the "Ted and Carol Show" now. When Carol started the session she was making statements about your staying at work, not being with the family, and not completing homework assignments. Imagine that she is still making the same statements. They sound pretty critical. In reality, since you are both "FMHBs," fallible messed-up human beings, you will sometimes be prone to communicate poorly and to blame each other. So, Carol is blaming you, and I'd like to show you how to choose to respond differently. Carol, go ahead and repeat what you said originally, and sound angry.

C: Ted, I've had it with you! You're more interested in helping clients than staying home with me and Stacia. You don't do your therapy homework. You don't take any initiative, and it just seems to me that you don't care!

T: Now what I am supposed to do?

EN: First, practice what Rogerian therapists call "**Active Listening.**" It involves giving back to the person what you just heard them say in an effort to make sure that you have accurately received the message that is being sent to you. So paraphrase for Carol what you have heard her say, and ask her if it's accurate, so that "message sent" does equal "message heard." You can begin with something like "What I heard you say . . ." or "So you're saying . . ." and then ask Carol if your understanding of what was said is accurate. Give her the opportunity to clarify if the message received is not 100 percent correct. Go ahead, give it shot.

T: Yeah, but I want to defend myself!

EN: Against what?

T: I'm being falsely accused and I'm starting to feel angry, even if we are just acting.

IT'S NOT AS BAD AS IT SEEMS

EN: Okay, right now let's identify your underlying irrational beliefs, like we have done in other sessions, and do some disputation in order to lower your distress level.

T: It's the anger and frustration shark again. I can actually hear myself thinking, "There she goes again accusing me! I can't stand it when she does that! She has no right to treat me that way!"

EN: Good, you've picked up on the iBs, the irrational beliefs. Now, how do you change those to rational beliefs?

T: You mean the "Where is it written" stuff?

EN: Yes.

T: I guess the disputation challenges would be, "Where is it written that she must not make such statements?" And the answer to that is, "Nowhere that I know of, even though I don't like it."

EN: Good. You mentioned frustration. What are the underlying irrational beliefs that create frustration?

T: The I-can't-stand-it-itis.

EN: And how are you going to dispute the I-can't-stand-it-itis?

T: If she makes statements that I don't like and even if she falsely accuses me, will it kill me? No, it won't kill me. Can I stand it? Yes, I can stand it, even though I will feel uncomfortable.

EN: So the new effects of disputing are . . . ?

T: While I would prefer that she not treat me that way and make those statements, she is who she is and she will sometimes say things I don't like. Tough! I can stand it, even though I don't like it at all.

EN: And how do you feel right now as you practice disputing the irrational beliefs?

133

IT'S NOT AS BAD AS IT SEEMS

T: Only annoyed with her reaction, not as angry.

EN: Let me offer a rule of thumb when it comes to relationship problems: First things first! In this case the first things that I'm talking about are getting my own irrational belief sharks in a row and back in their cages. If I don't detect and debate my own irrational beliefs first and change them to rational beliefs, then chances are my communication efforts will be less than effective and successful.

         Remember to ask yourself over and over again, "What am I telling myself right now?" Then you can determine whether your underlying beliefs and self-statements are likely to be part of the problem or part of the solution.

         Keep that video camera running so that you can have an accurate picture of your behaviors and actions. Are the actions part of the problem or part of the solution? In my opinion, this corner of the relationship foundation is crucial. In almost every case, we had better address our "stinking thinking" before we do anything else.

         Now, back at the effective communication ranch! Now that you've gotten your anger shark back in the cage, practice the active listening skills with Carol.

T: Carol, what I hear you saying is that you see me as being more interested in my clients than I am in you and Stacia. You're also saying that I haven't been doing much of the therapy homework, and that I haven't been taking much initiative, and that these things lead you to think that I don't care about you.

EN: Now, check it out with Carol to see if your replay is on target or not.

T: Is that what you're saying? Do I understand you correctly?

C: Yes, that's exactly what I'm saying.

IT'S NOT AS BAD AS IT SEEMS

EN: Carol, when Ted practices active listening and paraphrases your communication for you, how do you interpret it? I mean, some people think that this active listening stuff is silly. What's your impression?

C: It seems a little silly, but mostly because it's so different for us. We - I mean, I - just tend to react, and I'm off and running with my own interpretations, meanings, and conclusions. When Ted was restating what he heard me say, it helped me to really understand. If he's working hard enough to listen to what I'm saying, then I feel that what's being said by me is important. That, then, helps me to feel important. With those impressions, I have a hard time making myself angry.

EN: I want to take a minute and review what we have covered so far in this session. First, it is important that we make the personal commitment to detect our underlying irrational beliefs and other thinking errors, and start challenging and changing these before we do anything else. In fact, if you're feeling strongly angry or frustrated, I recommend that you keep your angry and frustrated mouth shut. Talk may be cheap in some situations, but once the words are out of your mouth, you can't buy them back no matter how hard you try! Statements made in anger and frustration linger. You have learned to use "time-outs" with Stacia as a way of consequenting her behavior, and you may want to take a time-out yourself if you're angry. In fact, either of you may ask for a time-out at any point. When you do, go for a walk or go into another part of the house and do some writing or thinking about your feelings and thoughts. When you take the time-out, agree in advance that you'll get back together at a specific time, preferably within the next hour or so.

Second, own your thinking, feeling, and actions. Use "I" statements instead of "you" accusations.

Third, practice active listening. It's a good idea to practice this regularly. During your five-minute dates, one of you can talk for a while and then the other can paraphrase and practice the active listening. Then, switch roles.

Fourth, remember to ask yourself, "How am I being part of the solution right this second?" Take that personal inventory of your thinking, feeling, and actions and see if they are part of the solution. If not, it is critical that you work your "thinking straight" therapy in order to be part of the solution and not part of the problem.

Finally, caring behaviors are to be added to the "Caring Days Inventory" often. I'd like you to add at least three or four each week. Working on caring behaviors is a lifelong home-work assignment. Caring behaviors change over time also. Dr. Hauck, in his book *The Three Faces of Love*, reminds us that we don't stop growing at age 18. Rather, we continue to go through a development process throughout our lives. As he points out, desires, wants, and wishes within a relationship tend to change every seven to ten years. It's not a "seven-year itch" as much as part of the growth process. However, if we don't share over time what our wants and wishes are within the relationship, what caring behaviors we'd like to experience, then we tend to pull or push apart from each other.

Carol and Ted were dedicated to maintaining and improving their relationship, and they worked hard in therapy. Bad habits do not develop overnight, and they don't change overnight.

Individuals and couples committed to change will need to stay in therapy as long as they and the therapist believe it necessary, to complete homework assignments in between therapy sessions such as reading books or other material on improving relationships, and to practice caring behaviors on a daily basis.

Have you ever wondered what would happen if you treated co-workers, business associates, customers, friends, or even strangers the way you treat your spouse or "significant other?" Chances are you wouldn't have many friends or customers, wouldn't be on the "best-liked list" at work, and might even get beat up by a stranger!

We exert the necessary energy (most of the time) when dealing with other people, but won't put forth the energy when it comes to the most important people in our lives! We seem to take them for granted and expect them to not only tolerate our bad moods, uproars, and inappropriate behavior, but also to be "understanding" of these moods and actions. It is as if we believe that there is a universal law that says that those individuals with whom we are involved in loving relationships **MUST** tolerate and **MUST** understand us when we act badly.

Rational thinking can certainly help the people in our lives to avoid disturbing themselves over our bad behavior. But remember, change starts with each of us individually. Sometimes, when I'm about to say something to my wife or a friend, I'll stop and ask myself, "Would I say what I'm about to say to a client, or a stranger?"

If the answer is "no," then I had better work diligently to keep my mouth shut and not say it to the person who is important to me. I can work on saying what I'm thinking in a more constructive and appropriate way. I can use "I" statements and avoid pointing my finger at and blaming the other person.

Communication Strategies

In the session with Carol and Ted, we reviewed some of the strategies that can be used to improve communication such as active listening, using "I" statements, and identifying our irrational thinking that interferes with the communication process.

There are some other specifics that you may find helpful:

(1)   Avoid dredging up all of the "old junk" from the past. Make an effort to keep your focus on the "here-and-now." If there is old junk from the past to be dealt with, maybe it would be a good idea to address these issues with a third party such as a therapist, a counselor, or a member of the clergy. There are issues from the past that may call for discussion, such as having a history of physical or sexual abuse, or having been reared in a family where there was alcohol abuse or dependency, since these are the types of concerns that can be influential in the development of the irrational belief sharks. In therapy or counseling these can be explored, and both people in the relationship can gain a better understanding of the irrational beliefs and how to change them.

137

IT'S NOT AS BAD AS IT SEEMS

(2)   Avoid thinking errors like mind-reading and fortune-telling. How often do you hear yourself thinking, "I know why she did that!" or "I know what she or he is thinking!" I agree with Dr. Beck, who wrote in *Love is Never Enough* that mind reading is probably one of the biggest thinking errors that contributes to relationship problems.

(3)   Sharpen your communication skills by avoiding certain hazards such as "drifting" (letting the topics change frequently without ever resolving or managing what was being discussed), "kitchen sinking" (throwing everything into the discussion including the kitchen sink), "yes, butting" (saying, "Yes, but you . . ."), "cross-complaining" (interrupting while your partner is talking), performing a "character assassination" (damning or condemning the person rather than describing the behavior or action), and the passive-aggressive trick of "pouting" (using silence as a weapon).[10]

(4)   Remember to put some politeness back into the relationship. Offer your partner sincere and positive appreciation. If you have an issue to resolve, schedule a time when you can sit down without interruptions, and work on managing the conflict or resolving the issue. Be considerate and courteous with this important person in your life. Express interest in your partner's activities, listen when he or she talks about these activities, and ask questions. In fact, ask lots of questions! Let the speaker finish completely rather than interrupting. Keep looking for the positive rather than trying to catch the negative. Condemn the sin and **NOT THE SINNER**. Damn the deed and **NOT THE DOER**. Other people's actions and behaviors can be judged, but remember that we as humans are in no position to judge other people. Be empathic and think about the other person's wants, wishes, and desires, rather than thinking about your own. Try to "get behind the other person's eyeballs" and see the world a little more like he or she does.[11]

I may be wrong, but I am personally and professionally convinced that a relationship can be improved when each person in the relationship will make the personal commitment to identify his or her contributions to the troubled relationship and, more importantly, to dedicate himself or herself to changing these bad habits. As I have said often in this book, it's simple, but not easy, and it is not an impossible dream.

IT'S NOT AS BAD AS IT SEEMS

How are your important relationships? Any areas for improvement? As a member of the FMHB Club, there are certainly at least one or two areas that could be improved. Take some time right now and think about those areas, and outline below the steps that you will take to improve your relationships.

CHAPTER EIGHT

"It's Like I'm Going to Die!":
Coping With Panic and An xiety

My life has been filled with many catastrophes - most of which never came true.

- Mark Twain (I think!)

"I think I'm losing my mind!"

"I'm always nervous and worried."

"I can't catch my breath. I know I'm having a heart attack!"

"I feel like I'm going to die!"

"I always feel uptight. Always sweating and shaking."

None of the people who have presented these complaints were dying, or losing their minds, or having heart attacks, or in any real danger. In each case, the person was suffering from some type of **anxiety problem.**

People with anxiety problems are not alone, even though they sometimes feel intensely alone. In fact, research conducted by the National Institutes of Mental Health revealed that anxiety problems are the most common types of psychological difficulties experienced by people in the USA, even more common than depression.[1]

Anxiety

Anxiety is different from fear. Fear is usually a reaction to a real or threatened danger, and when we feel afraid, most of the time there is good reason for the fear. **Anxiety**, on the other hand, is usually a reaction to an unreal or imagined danger. Anxiety can be viewed as **real anxiety**, or **neurotic anxiety**. Real anxiety involves some type of objective danger.[2] Anxiety is viewed as **neurotic** when it becomes unhealthy and problematic.

Real anxiety can be associated with fear in many ways. Fear is one of the emotions that we have that serves to protect us. I am afraid of snakes so when I'm the woods, I always watch where I'm walking and keep my eyes peeled for snakes. This fear helps to keep me safe. While I may feel afraid and fearful of snakes, I am not anxious or phobic.

Phobias

Phobias are persistent fears of particular objects or situations that result in the objects or situations being avoided, or being associated with intense feelings of anxiety. These fears or avoidance end up interfering with daily routines, usual social activities or relationships, or they activate marked distress in general.[3] While I don't like snakes, I don't avoid the woods or reptile houses at zoos, and I have handled harmless snakes on many occasions. If I avoided the woods and reptile houses because of an excessive anxiety and this interfered with my purusit of happiness, then I might have a snake phobia. Phobias have been identified as one type of anxiety problem.

In addition to specific phobias which represent one form of "neurotic" anxiety, there is another type of disorder, **agoraphobia**, which literally means "fear of the market place." Agoraphobics have intense fear of being in places from which it would be difficult or impossible to escape and may avoid going out of their houses. They may also avoid driving, public transportation, crowds, stores, shopping malls, theaters, elevators, and other open or closed spaces.[4] Agoraphobia can be paralyzing to the person who suffers from this type of anxiety problem.

Other Types of Anxiety Disorders

There are several other types of anxiety disorders:

Social phobia, a persistent fear of social situations in which the person might act in a way that would be embarrassing or humiliating;

Obsessive compulsive disorders, involving either recurrent or persistent ideas perceived as intrusive and senseless, compulsive behaviors, which are repetitive actions that are performed in response to an obsessive thought or designed to neutralize or prevent discomfort;

Post-traumatic stress disorder, anxiety and other symptoms develop following a distressing event such war experiences, car accidents, rape, etc.[5]

But the two types of anxiety problems I see most often are **panic attacks** and **generalized anxiety disorders.**

Panic attacks are described as a surge of anxiety that is usually unexpected and not related to a particular situation. At least four of the following symptoms are associated with panic attacks:

(1)   shortness of breath or a smothering sensation
(2)   dizziness or feeling faint
(3)   a racing heart beat
(4)   shaking or trembling
(5)   sweating
(6)   choking sensations
(7)   nausea or general stomach distress
(8)   feeling as if the situation is not real or feeling depersonalized, like it is not really "me"
(9)   numbness or tingling
(10)   hot flashes or chills
(11)   chest pain or discomfort in the chest
(12)   fear of dying
(13)   fear of doing something uncontrolled or fear of going crazy.[6]

Generalized anxiety involves unrealistic or excessive worry about two or more life circumstances for a period of at least six months, during which the person is bothered by the anxiety more days than not.

Specific symptoms of generalized anxiety include feeling shaky, muscle tension, restlessness, feeling tired, shortness of breath, rapid heart rate, sweating, dry mouth, feeling dizzy, nausea, hot flashes or chills, trouble swallowing, frequent urination, feeling keyed up, being easily startled, problems concentrating, sleep problems, and general irritability.[7]

Whenever clients come to see me for therapy, one of the first things that I do is to refer them for a comprehensive medical evaluation if they have not had one within the past six months to a year. As you read some of the symptoms above, you may have thought that these could be associated with physical problems.

If you did, you were right! People might well be feeling anxious or depressed, but the cause of these feelings might not be "stinking thinking" in all cases. Some people have thyroid problems, low or high blood sugar, or mild heart problems that can mimic psychological problems.

As you will read in the next therapy session, I believe that it is *very* important for clients to see a physician in order to eliminate the possibility of an underlying medical problem of some sort. While some people may have a physical or medical basis for their anxiety, most anxiety is related to thinking problems rather than medical problems.

It's Awful!

In this chapter you will meet Frank, who has problems with anxiety and panic. Frank is in his early forties, has a management job with a large company, and has been divorced for several years. When Frank was seen for his first session he described having had problems with anxiety for the past year. In addition to having chronic feelings of anxiety, he had in the past four months begun to have panic attacks.

During the first session he said that during the past month he had five "attacks," and now he found himself almost constantly worried about having another panic attack. Since his job required that he often give presentations, he was becoming increasingly anxious about giving these presentations because he anticipated having a panic attack while giving the talk, and this was beginning to interfere with his job performance.

The goal of therapy is to eliminate panic attacks and intense levels of anxiety that he feels. This is the second therapy session.

EN: Did you bring your Daily Mood Record with you?

F: Yeah. After keeping this for the past week, I think I'm more anxious than I thought I was. My anxiety level averaged about an "8" all week, and I had six panic attacks. I got a physical last week. The doctor said everything was fine. I guess I should be relieved by that, but in some ways I was disappointed. If there was something physically wrong, he could have just given me a pill or something and cured it.

EN: I think that is good news. Anxiety and panic problems are extremely common, and recent studies have shown that the type of therapy that you and I are going to do together is quite effective in eliminating anxiety problems. (Looking at the Daily Mood Record) I see that your anxiety level has been high. Was anything going on last week that might have been related to the "8" intensity?

F: Not that I can think of. It just seems like there is a constant sense of dread and anticipation that at any moment the anxiety will go even higher or that I will have a panic attack.

EN: So while there is no clear environmental or situational A or activator that you can put your finger on at this point, part of the activator seems to be the constant anticipation of problems.

F: I'd agree with that. It's like in the back of my mind, I'm always thinking that at any moment the panic may hit or the anxiety may completely take control of me.

EN: Even though we have not been able to give a very specific definition of the activator, would it be okay with you if we defined the A as thinking about the possibility of having a panic attack?

F: Sure, that makes sense to me.

EN: The emotional consequence, the C, is the anxiety that has averaged about an "8" all of last week, and at times the C has been the panic attacks. Any behaviors associated with the anxiety or panic?

F: I'm starting to shy away from presentations at work, which is not a good thing since my work evaluation is coming up next month. I had the opportunity recently to give a presentation to a group that would include one of the senior vice-presidents. It would have been a great chance for me to impress one of the people who will be evaluating me, but I said I was too busy and couldn't do it.

EN: Emotionally, then, you are feeling anxious and having panic attacks, and behaviorally avoiding certain situations and opportunities that could be self-enhancing.

F: Yes.

EN: Are there any other specifics that tend to be associated with the increased levels of anxiety or with the panic attacks?

F: Like what?

EN: Like do you ever have any physical sensations, heart racing, anything like that?

F: Heavens yes! Most of last week I kept noticing that I couldn't get my breath or that my heart was racing or that I felt a sense of tightness in my chest. I was glad you recommended that I get a comprehensive medical workup because in the past I was running to the emergency room or to a minor emergency clinic. They would give me a EKG or something, tell me I was fine, and that it was all in my head. In my head, my foot! Those are the worst sensations I have every experienced and I was certain that I was dying or would die real soon. At least last week since I had a full medical workup, I did know that I wasn't dying.

Many people spend thousands of dollars on trips to the emergency room convinced that they are dying, only to be told that the symptoms are "in their head." While we know that is factually correct in many cases, it often contributes to the problems that the person is experiencing while solutions such as seeking therapy or counseling are not always offered.

Many psychological problems may at first appear to be physical ailments. For example, people with depression or anxiety may complain of stomach problems, fatigue, muscle aches and pains, sleep problems, appetite and weight changes, back pain, headaches.

I believe that sometimes our bodies try to tell us something, but we may not know to listen. Rather than listen and view these sensations as friends and important information, we are prone to start upsetting ourselves which only makes the problem worse.

EN: We've identified the C and A. It's time to look for the B or belief associated with the anxiety and panic. What kinds of things go through your mind when you notice physical sensations like tightness in your chest or your heart pounding?

F: You remember the old television show "Sanford & Son" and how Fred Sanford when under stress used to look up at the heavens and say, "This is the big one Elizabeth, I'm coming to join you." Well, my thoughts are like that. I'm sure it's the beginning of the end, and that either death is just around the corner or, perhaps worse, a really big panic attack is just waiting to get me.

EN: So, you start thinking that you're going to die, have another panic attack, and what else goes through your head?

F: One thing that I think is "what if." What if something really is wrong with me and the doctors have just missed it! What if I have a major panic attack and really do die!

And "what ifs" are often associated with anxiety problems, just like "if onlys" tend to play some role in depression. The "what ifs" tend to suggest that you perceive some type of threat. Anxiety disorders almost always involve a sense of feeling vulnerable, a sense of threat to one's comfort, confidence, competence, or even self-esteem. The "what ifs" reflect some of the inferences we start to make. They may sound like questions but are really statements in disguise. What are the statements you're making to yourself when you start to have the physical sensations?

F: You mean, it is more than, "What if I'm having a heart attack?"

EN: Yes. That's a question. Turn the question into a statement.

F: I am having a heart attack!

EN: Right. That's the inference. And then what's the next thought? What do you say to yourself about having a heart attack?

F: I might die!

EN: And what would you think about that possibility?

F: That would be awful! That would really be catastrophic.

EN: When you start awfulizing and catastrophizing, how do you feel?

F: Silly question, doc! The more I awfulize, the more anxious I become. Probably the awfulizing and catastrophizing help to clear the path for a panic attack as well.

Catastrophic Misinterpretation

Bingo! Anxiety and panic disorders are becoming increasingly well understood thanks to extensive research that has been conducted. One of the factors that has been identified from this research is called **catastrophic misinterpretation.**[8] It tends to provide mental health professionals with one method of differentiating generalized anxiety from panic attacks.

People who suffer from panic attacks tend to report dramatic misinterpretations of their somatic sensations such as racing heart, tightness in the chest, and so on. In eliminating panic episodes, it is important to learn that our physical sensations are not dangerous and to learn to anti-catastrophize about them.

EN: Intellectually you know that you are not having a heart attack and that you are healthy, right?

F: It certainly seems so. I think I've had every test imaginable run on me, and all the results come back normal.

EN: Then it seems relatively safe to say that the anxiety and panic attacks are created at point B, your beliefs about the physical sensations. You've already done a good job of identifying the stinking thinking as awfulizing, terribleizing, and catastrophizing. In fact you just said that the belief is that you might have a heart attack, you might die, and that would be awful. From our earlier sessions, do you remember what the definition of "awful" is?

F: I think I remember you saying that awful means 100 percent bad or even 101 percent bad.

EN: When you are awfulizing and catastrophizing, what you are believing is that the sensations and the possibilities of having a heart attack or even of dying is 100 percent bad. Sticking with the physical sensations for a minute, when you have the tightness in your chest, sweating, shortness of breath, and other such symptoms, are they in fact 100 percent bad?

F: At the moment they sure seem that way!

EN: Having experienced the symptoms myself, I agree that they are pretty uncomfortable and certainly unpleasant, but are they 100 percent bad? Are the sensations worse than maybe having some type of very painful illness?

F: Well, no.

EN: Are the sensations the worse thing that could possibly happen to you?

F: No.

EN: Have you ever heard or read of any person dying simply because he or she experienced some unpleasant physical sensations? Ever heard of a death certificate that read, "Cause of death: sweating, tightness in chest, and other unpleasant physical sensations?"

F: Can't say that I have.

EN: But, Frank what happens is that you start to experience some physical sensations, and in all likelihood these sensations are normal, natural occurrences. Maybe you had one cup of coffee too many, or maybe your adrenaline is pumping a little more because you're anticipating a meeting with your boss. Your stinking thinking then automatically kicks in and you start jumping to conclusions and awfulizing. Maybe you start thinking, "Oh, my gosh, here it comes again! There's that tightness in my chest and I'm sweating. I **know** something is wrong with me! I just know that I'm having a heart attack. This is unbearable! It's absolutely awful and terrible!" And the more you misinterpret the sensations and catastrophize about them, the more your anxiety increases and the greater the likelihood of having a panic attack. Does this seem to make sense?

F: While I'm sitting here pretty relaxed it does. But when it happens, it all seems so automatic and like I can't control it.

EN: When you're driving and the stop light turns yellow, what do you usually do?

F: I slow down and prepare to stop since the yellow light means that the light is about to turn red.

EN: Right. Is the yellow light in any way dangerous to you?

F: No, in fact, it's helpful. It's a warning signal.

EN: Right. And so are the physical sensations that you experience. They are just warning signals just like the yellow light. When you see the yellow light, you don't go running for cover somewhere or hide in the trunk of your car. You view the yellow light in an objective, scientific fashion. Your outlook about the yellow light is realistic and reasonable. How might you start thinking of your physical sensations like you think of yellow lights?

F: I could think to myself, "Hmmm, my chest is a little tight right now and I'm sweating a little more than usual. Maybe I better slow down some and see what's going on. These sensations are just warning signs. They aren't dangerous, and they certainly can't hurt me."

EN: That's fantastic. And what about the awfulizing? Are the sensations truly 100 percent bad?

F: If I apply the disputation techniques that we've talked about, I realize that there is no scientific proof or evidence that the sensations are 100 percent bad. They're hardly as bad as having a serious physical illness. They are uncomfortable and bad, but not awful and unbearable. Obviously I have been able to stand them many times before, and I can stand them again. I also realize that there is no benefit in continually telling myself how awful they are, since awfulizing just makes the anxiety worse.

Empirical and Pragmatic Disputation

Frank has just applied two specific disputation techniques in eliminating his awfulizing and catastrophizing. What were they?

By looking for proof and hard scientific evidence to support the belief that the physical sensations are awful, terrible, and catastrophic, he is applying the **empirical** disputation approach. He also begins questioning the practical value of maintaining the belief that having the sensations is awful. This is the **practical** or **pragmatic** disputation technique.

In coping with anxiety and panic, there are several strategies that can be applied, as you will learn in this chapter. In Rational-Emotive Therapy and other cognitive behavioral approaches to thinking straight, an emphasis is placed on uncovering the irrational beliefs and distorted inferences. Awfulizing is almost always associated with anxiety problems, and it is important to get this irrational belief shark back in its cage in order to eliminate anxiety problems.

Frank is correct when he said that his thinking associated with the sensations is automatic. In earlier chapters, we discussed how many types of behaviors, actions, and thinking become automatic. Tying shoes becomes automatic, walking becomes automatic, and many times awfulizing also becomes automatic. The goal of therapy is to replace the bad habit of awfulizing with a much better habit of anti-awfulizing and rational thinking.

Let's return to the therapy session and see how Frank can begin to develop the new habit of rational thinking.

EN: Frank, would you be willing right now to keep working on your tendency to catastrophically misinterpret your physical sensations?

F: Sure, I think that would be a good idea.

EN: Good. Right now imagine that you are scheduled to give a presentation in about an hour. Also, imagine that you begin to have the physical sensation of tightness in your chest, your heart is beating rapidly, and you are beginning to perspire. Close your eyes right now and imagine that as vividly as you can.

F: (Frank closes his eyes.) Okay, it's not hard for me to get a mental image of that. I'm sitting in my office, looking at the clock, and realizing that in less than an hour I'm giving this presentation to the big bosses.

IT'S NOT AS BAD AS IT SEEMS

EN: And how are you starting to feel?

F: Even as I imagine the situation, I notice that I'm starting to feel anxious.

EN: Can you also begin to imagine, or even better, experience some of the physical sensations?

F: Yes, in fact, I notice right now that my heart is starting to beat faster than usual and I do feel the tension.

EN: So, right now you're beginning to pick up on sensations and noticing the emotional consequences of anxiety.

F: Yes.

EN: And what are the beliefs going through your head as you feel the anxiety and experience the physical sensations?

F: They're the "Here it comes again" thoughts. I just know I'm going to have a panic attack, and I can't stand it! These feelings are awful!

EN: So the automatic awfulizing thoughts have kicked in?

F: Yes, and I can see how my thinking that the sensations are awful are related to the feelings of anxiety.

EN: As you continue to imagine the scene right now, begin to challenge and dispute the awfulizing irrational beliefs, and do it out loud.

F: I know I'm telling myself right now that the sensations are awful, but are they 100 percent bad? No, while they are uncomfortable, they're not unbearable. Will I die from these feelings? No way! I can stand them even though I don't like them.

EN: Good, you're showing that right now you are able to dispute the irrational beliefs and also, as a result of the disputing, replace the automatic awfulizing irrational beliefs with rational alternatives. As you're doing that, what do you notice happening to the feelings?

F: (Frank opens his eyes.) My anxiety really begins to go down. Even as I imagined the scene, I was feeling an anxiety level that was close to an "8." As I began detecting the irrational beliefs and disputing them, and, more importantly, replacing the irrational beliefs with rational alternatives, I began to feel much less anxious and only mildly concerned.

EN: Terrific! I really think you're on your way to getting your anxiety sharks back in their cages and keeping them there. What I would like for you do to over the next week is to pay careful attention to your bodily "yellow lights." When you start to have some of the physical sensations which have in the past been associated with the anxiety and panic, immediately start looking for the awfulizing and begin challenging and disputing these underlying irrational beliefs. Also take time to write down the specific emotional and behavioral consequences, the intensity of these emotions, any specific activators associated with the feelings, and the particular underlying irrational beliefs. Then write down the specific disputation questions used to combat this irrational thinking. As you effectively dispute the irrational beliefs, notice how the feelings change and write down the changes that you notice. Would you be willing to do that, Frank?

F: Sure, I want to do whatever it takes.

Packing Your Psychological Suitcase

As Frank begins to practice detecting and disputing the irrational beliefs associated with the anxiety and panic, he will most likely notice a dramatic reduction in his feelings of anxiety as well as a reduction in the frequency and intensity of his panic attacks.

In addition to applying the Rational-Emotive thinking straight techniques for managing and eliminating anxiety, I want to help Frank "pack a psychological suitcase" with other strategies that will also be useful when he experiences the intense anxiety and the panic episodes.

IT'S NOT AS BAD AS IT SEEMS

Whether helping clients deal with anxiety, panic, depression, anger, or frustration, one of the first steps is to provide education. In Frank's case, it was important to educate him about anxiety and panic. This included familiarizing him with the symptoms associated with anxiety and panic, and assuring him with the fact that these symptoms are quite common, that they are not dangerous, and, more importantly, that Frank can master these symptoms.

One of the ways to learn more about psychological problems is to read books and pamphlets that have been written on the various types of problems. While a number of good books have been written about anxiety and panic, I have found a book written by Drs. David Barlow and Michelle Craske entitled, *Mastery of Your Anxiety and Panic*, to be extremely helpful.[9] Information on ordering this useful resource is available in the reference section for this chapter.

Relaxation Training

In packing that psychological suitcase, it's also nice to have some behavioral techniques that could be used along with the thinking straight strategies. One technique that is extremely helpful is **relaxation training**.

In addition to awfulizing, another symptom that is almost always associated with anxiety, especially with panic, is a state of general **physical tension**.

Research on panic disorders has indicated that along with catastrophic misinterpretation, another factor associated with panic attacks is the tendency to **hyperventilate**. As a result of hyperventilation, people reduce their oxygen intake and increase the build-up of carbon dioxide. Relaxation training and breathing retraining can be effective ways of reducing the general tension associated with anxiety and panic.

In this next portion of the therapy session, I will introduce Frank to some of the methods for reducing the physical tension.

EN: In addition to disputing your underlying irrational beliefs, I would also like to introduce you to some other techniques

154

that you can use when you're experiencing intense anxiety and panic attacks. When you're experiencing anxiety, and especially panic episodes, what's your breathing like?

F: My breathing is almost always very rapid, almost like I'm hyperventilating.

EN: This is common among people who experience debilitating anxiety, and it's almost always a factor in panic attacks. Chances are that as your breathing becomes more and more rapid, it seems that your anxiety will increase dramatically.

F: You're right, it really does.

EN: So let me introduce you to a technique for gaining better control over your breathing. Close your eyes. Sit comfortably, and begin to relax. What I want you to do is, on one, I want you to breathe in through your nose and think, "Relax." On two, breathe out through your mouth, and again think, "Relax." As you're breathing in on one, you're inhaling the relaxation, and as you breathe out on two, you're exhaling the tension and general discomfort. Let's try it right now. One . . . breathe in relaxation . . . and two . . . exhale the tension, anxiety, and distress. Keep doing that right now as you say to yourself, "One, breathe in relaxation, two, exhale the tension and distress." Keep practicing it right now.

Frank was encouraged to continue practicing this relaxation strategy for approximately three or four minutes. He indicated that he found the technique helpful. He was encouraged to focus his attention on his breathing and his counting, breathe deeply from his diaphragm, and keep his chest still.

EN: Now I want to show you another technique that you can use in order to reduce your physical tension. I want you to tense every muscle in your body right now. Make a fist with both hands, push your feet down against the floor so that you tighten all the muscles in your legs, thighs, shins, and hips, tighten the muscles in your chest and stomach, tighten the

muscles in your arms, and in your face, head, and neck.
Just work to tighten all the muscles in your body, make them
as tight as you can, right now. Notice that tension. Notice
how uncomfortable that feeling is. Now relax. Just let all of
the muscles in your body relax, and feel that tension that you
just created being replaced with a warm wave of relaxation
and comfort. Frank, notice the difference between the
feeling of tension and the feeling of relaxation that you've
just created. As you experience the relaxation flowing
through your body, continue to practice, breathing in on
one, and thinking "Relax" and exhaling on two, as you
replace the tension with relaxation. How is the relaxation
training and breathing retraining working for you right now,
Frank?

F: This is great! I can really see how I can use these strategies
        when I start to feel tense and anxious!

Relaxation training, including "Breathing Retraining" and
"Progressive Muscle Relaxation,"[10] are extremely useful in learning
to control and manage relaxation, and learning how to control
anxiety and panic. Like any other skills, these techniques can only
be learned after a great deal of practice and rehearsal.

Frank was encouraged to practice relaxation at least twice a
day, preferably once during the day and once before bedtime.
Using the relaxation strategies, he found that he was even able to
sleep better than he had in the past.

A number of bookstores carry relaxation tapes, and some of
these tapes can be purchased from the Institute for Rational-Emotive
Therapy in New York (for a copy of the publications available from
the Institute, write: Institute for Rational-Emotive Therapy, 45 E.
65th Street, New York, NY 10021). Other specific relaxation
strategies are outlined in the workbook, *Mastery of Your Anxiety
and Panic.*

Distraction

Another technique that can be used in the midst of an anxiety
or panic attack is *"Distraction."* What too often happens is that

when people begin to experience intense feelings of anxiety or panic, they become totally immersed in the discomfort of the symptoms. One option is to redirect your focus from the uncomfortable anxiety symptoms and momentarily distract yourself by focusing on something else.

For instance, if you suddenly began to have panic symptoms while in a room full of people, you could stop and ask yourself how many people in the room have blond hair. You might also ask yourself how many people were wearing sweaters, or how many men or women were in the room. You might also count the number of objects hung on the wall, or how many people were smiling at that moment.

Any such strategy can be used to distract yourself from the anxiety or panic symptoms, and this technique has been found to be especially useful in reducing the extreme distress associated with panic attacks. This is true because panic attacks represent the sudden surge of the intense anxiety, terror, or fear for no apparent reason, accompanied by some of the symptoms described earlier, including difficulty breathing, trembling, sweating, and chest pain. During this intense discomfort, the ability to redirect one's focus from these symptoms to other elements of one's environment can be beneficial.

Medication

With Frank, I used thinking straight techniques, relaxation training, breathing retraining, and distraction techniques. What about medication? Is that something that would benefit Frank?

Decisions regarding medication are made between clients and their physicians. In some cases, for example, individuals who have both a severe depression as well as an anxiety disorder may benefit from certain types of medication. However, many people who experience anxiety and panic are too often treated with antianxiety medications without the benefit of therapy or counseling. Some of these medications can be addicting and abused and can become part of the problem rather than part of the solution.

IT'S NOT AS BAD AS IT SEEMS

People considering medication should discuss possible side effects openly with their physicians, and should also question their physician about the potential for abuse of the medication, including becoming addicted to it. The physician should also be questioned about the likelihood of the anxiety or panic symptoms returning following the discontinuation of the medication.

One study has recently suggested that one form of therapy based on cognitive behavior therapy is more effective in eliminating panic attacks than is antianxiety medication.[11]

In therapy, Frank worked hard and quickly learned the techniques necessary for reducing his generalized anxiety, and also eliminating his panic attacks. By keeping his Daily Mood Record, both he and I were able to see how successfully he reduced his anxiety. Being a fallible human being, there were episodes in which his anxiety would increase, but we were able to use his Mood Record to uncover specific activators and to tap into his underlying irrational beliefs and faulty inferences.

Very quickly, he eliminated his panic attacks, since he began to recognize the early warning signals. Rather than catastrophizing about these sensations, he was able to think rationally about them and therefore avoid the escalation of the anxiety, eventually resulting in the panic.

He found that by practicing relaxation training and deep breathing exercises several times a day, he gained a greater sense of control, which was useful in reducing the generalized anxiety. He completed his therapy after approximately 15 sessions, with the last five or six sessions being "follow-up" and "booster" sessions.

In working with clients, I find it helpful to schedule such follow-up and booster sessions as a routine part of therapy. Rather than believing that therapy "must" take place on a weekly basis for "x" number of weeks, I believe that each individual is unique and that therapy can be structured to meet the individual wants and needs of each person. Following perhaps six to 12 weekly sessions, the scheduled appointments can be less frequent in an effort to provide the individual the opportunity to practice the skills that are learned within therapy.

I remind people that therapy is only 45 minutes to one hour out of a 168-hour week, and that positive change will rapidly take place if homework assignments are completed between sessions. By spacing therapy sessions to every other week, or perhaps once a month, more time is provided for practice. In some cases, I see certain people for quarterly sessions, or even once a year.

As we say "goodbye" to Frank, his anxiety, and his panic, I'd like for you to put on your "therapist hat" again and think about yourself. Have you ever been troubled by anxiety? Have you ever had a panic attack?

Since more than 30 percent of the population in the United States has experienced some sort of panic attack in the past year, if you have, you are certainly not alone.[12]

Suggested Homework for Chapter Eight:

Are there certain times or certain events that tend to be more associated with anxiety than other times or events? The last time you felt particularly anxious, what were the self-statements and thoughts going through your head?

How did you handle this anxiety? Was it healthy, such as applying rational thinking? Was it unhealthy, such as using alcohol or other nonprescription drugs in the effort to reduce the anxiety? Remember that people who have problems with anxiety frequently turn to alcohol and other drugs, and in the process develop another problem associated with alcohol or drug abuse, or even dependency.

Take some time right now and reflect on the questions I've just asked, and, if you have had problems with anxiety and panic, write down some of your thoughts, reactions, and goals.

CHAPTER NINE

Declining Invitations to Pity Parties:
How to Avoid Backsliding

Nobody can make you feel inferior without your consent.

- Eleanor Roosevelt

This book is about choices. While we often don't choose the things that happen to us, we do choose our outlooks. We can't control the weather, but we can control how we think about the weather. To once more paraphrase Epictetus, "I am disturbed not by things, but by the views I take of them."

In many ways, this book has also been about how to say "no" to certain invitations. Events, people, places, and things may at times invite us to feel self-pity, depression, anger, or other negative and inappropriate emotions. But most invitations include a R.V.S.P., and this means that we can either accept the invitation or decline it. The invitations, if such were really mailed out, would look like the one below.

Dear_____
(Insert your name here.)

You   are   cordially   invited

TO: *Make yourself feel depressed, miserable, anxious and frustrated.*

Love and kisses,

_____
(Whoever is sending the invitation)
RSVP

160

IT'S NOT AS BAD AS IT SEEMS

Throughout life, you will receive invitations to pity parties, anger parties, anxiety parties, frustration parties, and general misery parties. Before you read this book, you may have believed that when invited, you were compelled to accept the invitation to misery.

But now you know, it ain't so! No matter what your mother, father, wife, husband, boss, or friend has told you in the past, or tells you today, you do have a choice. You can say no to these invitations by changing your outlook and developing a set of healthy, rational beliefs. Now you know you can always decline the invitation to misery, **NO MATTER WHAT!**

After reading this book, it is my hope that you have developed new insight and understanding. In fact, there are three insights that I hope you have gained:

Rational-Emotive Therapy Insight Number One:

Upset and emotional disturbance comes not from past events, but from our irrational thinking and beliefs that we maintain about these events. This insight is what we have referred to as the "B-C Connection," which emphasizes that beliefs largely create emotional and behavioral consequences.

Rational-Emotive Therapy Insight Number Two:

No matter how we originally became or made ourselves disturbed or upset, we have those feelings today because we are still "brainwashing" ourselves, that is, telling ourselves the same old garbage over and over again, with the same irrational beliefs that we developed in the past.

Rational-Emotive Therapy Insight Number Three:

Even when we achieve Insights Number One and Number Two, and realize that we have created and keep carrying on our own disturbed feelings and behaviors, this knowledge will not automatically result in change. Only if we constantly work and practice in the present and future to think, feel, and act against our irrational beliefs are we likely to put the sharks of irrational thinking in their cages and generally keep them there.[1]

Backsliding

I believe that the work and practice insight is most important. The goal is not just to "feel better," but rather to get better and stay better. As you read this book and did your homework, you may have learned a lot about your underlying irrational beliefs, and may have made considerable positive change.

If that's the case, congratulations! But, guess what?

Because you are human, you will most likely backslide, and you may even slide far back. Remember Ruth in Chapter Six? She did some backsliding and was able to learn that this was just more evidence that she was human and therefore imperfect.

Dr. Ellis has presented some important information on how to maintain and enhance the Rational-Emotive Therapy gains that you have made.[2] When we backslide, it doesn't mean that we have failed, it simply means that we have an opportunity to practice what we have learned.

If you backslide, identify the specific thoughts, feelings, and behaviors that you once changed in order to bring about improvement. Remind yourself that you were able to do it in the past and that you can do it again. You have the skills, and you can do it. You may not be successful at first, but when you keep practicing and working hard, success can follow.

With force and passion, push rational beliefs and coping statements through your head. For example, if you feel depressed and recognize that you are self-downing, make the statement, "I accept myself unconditionally, and because I fail at things does not make me a failure!" Don't make these statements in a wimpy, namby-pamby fashion, but rather, be enthusiastic and forceful and passionate!

If you backslide, go fishing for sharks. Remember that the irrational beliefs are responsible for the inappropriate negative feelings, and that you can identify these sharks and begin disputing and challenging the underlying irrational beliefs. Review Chapters Four and Five on getting the sharks back in their cages by using disputation techniques.

If you find yourself in some of the "old behaviors" that were defeating, such as avoiding situations or not acting assertively, be willing to take risks and to force yourself to do some of the things that you are avoiding. Remind yourself that while you may feel uncomfortable, you will be able to stand it.

Be careful not to mislabel very appropriate yet uncomfortable and negative feelings as signs of failure. You will surely have negative feelings such as sadness, annoyance, irritation, and regret, but these feelings are quite appropriate and healthy, since they rarely interfere with our pursuit of happiness.

As was mentioned in earlier chapters, people often down themselves because of negative feelings, which can turn appropriate sadness into inappropriate depression. Be careful not to let an appropriate negative emotion become an activator for irrational thinking, which will then create the defeating emotional and behavioral consequences.

Whether you backslide or not, be nice to yourself (and others). Find healthy ways of rewarding yourself and be kind to yourself. When you are nice to yourself, it is much easier to be nice to those around you.

The S-H-A-R-K

In Chapter 3, I said that the **S-H-A-R-K** was not only a way of thinking about irrational beliefs, but that it also had special meaning. Each of the letters stands for something, and you can "think **S-H-A-R-K**" whenever you are dealing with a situation that is triggering unhealthy feelings, actions, and thinking. When you do, you will be reminded of how to change an irrational belief to a rational way of thinking.

IT'S NOT AS BAD AS IT SEEMS

S   **Stinking,** self-defeating self-talk and beliefs.

H   **Hold** it!! You've got choices now! What do you want to do?

A   **Attack** the irrational belief and use your disputing and debating skills.

R   **Replace** with rational beliefs. You've done it, so now

K   **Keep** up the good work and give yourself a pat on the back.

Read and Listen to Tapes

Dr. Ellis and other Rational-Emotive and Cognitive-Behavioral Therapists have written many helpful books that can help you maintain your improvement and avoid backsliding. (Buying the books and putting them under your pillow at night won't help much! Remember, if you buy the books, to read them after you have bought them.) Since I suffer from low frustration tolerance, I have found that listening to audio tapes is a great way of identifying and managing my irrational belief sharks. The Institute for Rational Emotive Therapy (45 E. 65th Street, New York, NY 10021) can provide you with a catalog that lists all of the books and audio tapes that are available. Some of the audio tapes that I have found helpful include *Conquering Low Frustration Tolerance, Rational Living in an Irrational World, RET and Assertiveness Training, Unconditionally Accepting Yourself and Others,* and *Conquering the Dire Need for Love* just to name a few of the tapes by Dr. Ellis that are available from the Institute. I strongly encourage you to use these and other tapes and books.

In addition to these books and pamphlets, take time to look over the material in the Appendix. I have included some handout material that you may find helpful.

Using the RET Self-Help Form

Dr. Joyce Sichel and Dr. Ellis have developed the *RET Self-Help Form* and a copy of this form is included in the Appendix section of this book. I recommend that my clients use this form, and I have used the form personally many times when caging my irrational belief sharks. At least one time each day (preferably many times each day!), select a situation in which you found yourself feeling disturbed and emotionally upset. Use the *Self-Help Form* to identify the activators, emotional and behavioral consequences, and the irrational beliefs associated with the undesirable emotions and actions. Then use the form to start to forcefully dispute the circled irrational beliefs. Successful disputing will lead to new effective beliefs that in turn will result in new feelings and behaviors that are healthy and helpful.

Over the years I have noticed that some people do better with different types of self-help forms. So, I have come up with two different self-help forms, and both of these are included in the Appendix section of the book. The self-help form called "RET FORM #2" also has an instruction sheet that is included.

Practicing with Others

Another suggestion that Dr. Ellis gives is to stay in touch with people who know something about Rational-Emotive Therapy and the thinking straight approach. I would suggest that you form a study group or a book club. In meetings, the group can discuss books, articles, pamphlets, or tapes which present more information about Rational-Emotive Therapy.

There may be professionals in your area who have been trained in Rational-Emotive Therapy who could even give a talk on a topic related to RET. By contacting the Institute for Rational-Emotive Therapy, you can obtain a list of institute-trained therapists and supervisors and a catalog of available resources.

Practice using the "thinking straight approach" not only with yourselves, but also with others. Maybe a friend is complaining of feeling angry, and you hear statements like, "He really made me angry!" Take the opportunity to start teaching your friend about the ABC's of RET. This doesn't mean that you become the person's therapist. In fact, be sensitive to the importance of referring a person with problems to a trained mental health professional, physician, or member of the clergy.

165

IT'S NOT AS BAD AS IT SEEMS

Continuing the Journey

In order to avoid backsliding, I recommend viewing change as a lifelong homework assignment. It would be beneficial to continue to write in your personal journal or therapy log, and to record various examples when you apply rational thinking to problems.

It would also be helpful to continue to keep the Daily Mood Record, and this could serve both to alert you to potential problems and to act as a clear indicator of how well you are doing in applying your rational thinking skills.

You will continue in the journey of thinking straight for your entire life. As you travel, you will be drawing a map that will be used in your pursuit of happiness, achievement of goals, and effective living. Many of us are using "maps" that are outdated, obsolete, and perhaps even dangerous. It would be like using a map of a large city that had been drawn 30 years ago. You would not be able to find many of the streets and locations that you would need, and you would frequently find yourself lost. You may get lost from time to time using the rational thinking map, but at least you will know that you can use your skills to get back on the right path.

Suggested Homework for Chapter Nine:

For your final homework assignment, I would like you to think about your goals. It is preferable to be solution-oriented and goal-oriented rather than being problem-oriented.

In the space below, write down the major "problems" that you perceive in your life. Remember to keep the focus on personal ownership of your own thinking, feeling, and behavior, rather than on blaming others. Be as specific and concrete as possible in identifying these problem areas:

Next, what are your goals? How will you know that the problems you have identified have been effectively managed? What will be the thinking, feeling, and behaving steps that you will take in order to manage or resolve the problems identified?

What obstacles can you imagine will interfere with your achievement of your goals? How can you apply Rational-Emotive Therapy to help eliminate these road blocks?

Remember that change can be a slow process, and that old habits die hard. Be patient and accepting of yourself and others, and remember that ongoing work and practice will be necessary for change. Best of success to you during your positive change journey, and remember to . . .

HAVE A RATIONAL DAY!

REFERENCES

CHAPTER ONE

1:     Covey, Stephen R. *The Seven Habits of Highly Effective People.* New York, NY: Simon & Schuster, 1989.

2.   Ibid, p. 31

3:     Young, Howard S. *A Rational Counseling Primer.* New York, NY: Institute for Rational-Emotive Therapy, 1974.

CHAPTER TWO

1:     Maultsby, Maxie C. *Rational Behavior Therapy.* Englewood Cliffs, NJ: Prentice-Hall, Inc., 1984.

2:     Wessler, Richard L., and Hankin-Wessler, Sheenah W.R. *Cognitive Appraisal Therapy* (CAT). In: Windy Dryden and William Golden (eds.), Cognitive-Behavioural Approaches to Psychotherapy. New York, NY: Harper & Rowe Publishers, 1986.

3:     Dryden, Windy *Rational-Emotive Therapy: Fundamentals and Innovations.* London: Croom Helm, 1984. (Much of the material in this chapter can be found in Dr. Dryden's book.)

CHAPTER THREE

1:     Dryden, Windy, and DiGiuseppe, Raymond. *A Primer on Rational-Emotive Therapy.* Champaign, IL: Research Press, 1990. (Much of this chapter is based on the information presented in this text.)

2:     Ibid.

3:     Ellis, Albert. *How to Stubbornly Refuse to Make Yourself Miserable About Anything - Yes, Anything!* Secaucus, NJ: Lyle Stewart, Inc., 1988.

4:     Dryden & DiGiuseppe, 1990. op cit.

5:      Wessler, Richard. Personal communication, July 18, 1981.

6:      Beck, Aaron T.; Rush, A. John; Shaw, Brian F.; and Emery, Gary. *Cognitive Therapy of Depression.* New York, NY: The Gillford Press, 1979.

7:      Burns, David D. *Feeling Good: The New Mood Therapy.* New York, NY: New American Library, 1980.

8:      Burns, David D. *The Feeling Good Handbook.* New York, NY: William Morrow & Company, Inc., 1989.

9:      Ellis, Albert. Forward: Written by Ellis, Albert & Dryden, Windy. In: Dryden, Windy. *Rational-Emotive Therapy: Fundamentals and Innovations.* London: Croom Helm, 1984.

10:     Burns, David D., 1989. op cit.

CHAPTER FOUR

1:      Dryden, Windy, and DiGiuseppe, Raymond. *A Primer on Rational-Emotive Therapy.* Champaign, IL: Research Press, 1990. (Much of this chapter is based on this text, as well as a workshop presented by Dr. DiGiuseppe on June 14, 1990.)

2:      Some of these questions came from: Persons, J.B. (1989). *Cognitive Therapy in Practice: A Case Formulation Approach.* New York: W.W. Norton, Inc.

CHAPTER FIVE

1:      American Psychiatric Association. *Diagnostic and Statistical Manual of Mental Disorders* (Third Edition - Revised). Washington, D.C.: American Psychiatric Association, 1987.

2:      Regier, Darrel A., Boyd, Jeffrey H., Burke, Jack D., Rae, Donald S., Myers, Jerome K., Kramer, Morton, Robins, Lee N., George, Linda K., Karno, Marvin, and Locke Ben Z. One-month prevalence of mental disorders in the United States. *Archives of General Psychiatry,* 45, 977-986, 1988.

3:      Rapee, Ronald. The psychological treatment of panic attacks: Theoretical conceptualization and review of evidence. *Clinical Psychology Review,* 7, 427 - 438.

4:      Dryden, Windy. *Dealing with Anger Problems: Rational-Emotive Therapeutic Interventions.* Sarasota, FL: Professional Resource Exchange, Inc., 1990.

CHAPTER SIX

1:      The Daily Mood Record is based on a form developed by David H. Barlow, Ph.D. and Michelle G. Craske, Ph.D. in their book, *Mastery of Your Anxiety and Panic.*

2:      Ellis, Albert. *Techniques for disputing irrational beliefs* (DIBS). New York, NY: Institute for Rational-Emotive Therapy, 1974.

3:      Ellis, Albert. *Emotional disturbance and its treatment in a nutshell.* New York, NY: Institute for Rational-Emotive Therapy, 1974.

4:      Beck, Aaron T., and Greenberg, Ruth L. *Coping with depression.* New York, NY: Institute for Rational-Emotive Therapy, 1974.

5:      Maultsby, Maxie C., and Ellis, Albert. *Techniques for using Rational-Emotive Imagery* (REI). New York, NY: Institute for Rational-Emotive Therapy, 1974.

6:      Golden, William. Personal communication, January 29, 1982. I modified this somewhat.

7:      Ellis, Albert. *How to maintain and enhance your rational-emotive therapy gains.* New York, NY: Institute for Rational-Emotive Therapy, 1984.

CHAPTER SEVEN

1:      Beck, Aaron T. *Love Is Never Enough.* New York, NY: Harper & Rowe Publishers, 1988.

2:     Hauck, Paul. *The Three Faces of Love*. Philadelphia: Westminster Press, 1984.

3:     Ellis, Albert, and Harper, Robert A. *A New Guide to Rational Living*. North Hollywood, CA: Wilshire Book Company, 1961.

4:     Ellis, Albert. *How to Live with a Neurotic*. New York: Crown, Revised Edition, 1975.

5:     Stuart, Richard B., and Jacobson, Barbara. Increasing caring behaviors. In: Stuart, Richard B., and Jacobson, Barbara. *Couple's Therapy Workbook* (Revised Edition). Champaign, IL: Research Press, 1987.

6:     Ibid.

7:     Ibid.

8:     Stuart, Richard B. *Helping Couples Change*. New York, NY: The Gillford Press, 1980.

9:     Ibid.

10:    The communication guidelines presented in this chapter are from Gottman, John; Notarius, Cliff; Gonso, Jonni; and Markman, Howard. *A Couple's Guide to Communication*. Champaign, IL: Research Press, 1976.

11:    Ibid.

CHAPTER EIGHT

1:     Regier, Darrel A., Boyd, Jeffrey H., Burke, Jack D., Rae, Donald S., Myers, Jerome K., Kramer, Morton, Robins, Lee N., George, Linda K., Karno, Marvin, and Locke Ben Z. One-month prevalence of mental disorders in the United States. *Archives of General Psychiatry,* 45, 977-986, 1988.

2.   Freeman, Arthur, and Ludgate John W. Cognitive therapy of anxiety: A clinical guide. In Keller, Peter A., and Heyman Steven R. (eds.), *Innovations in Clinical Practice: A*

Source Book. Sarasota, FL: Professional Resource Exchange, Inc., 1988.

2:     American Psychiatric Association. *Diagnostic and Statistical Manual of Mental Disorders* (Third Edition - Revised).

3:     Ibid.

4:     Ibid.

5:     Ibid.

6:     Ibid.

7:     Ibid.

8:     Rapee, Ronald. The psychological treatment of panic attacks: Theoretical conceptualization and review of evidence. *Clinical Psychology Review*, 7, 427 - 438.

9:     Barlow, David H., and Craske, Michelle G. *Mastery of Your Anxiety and Panic.* Center for Stress and Anxiety Disorders, University of Albany, State University of New York, 1989. To order this book, contact: Dr. David Barlow, Center for Stress and Anxiety Disorders, 1535 Western Avenue, Albany, New York 12203. Address any correspondence to ATTN: Graywind Publications.

10:     Ibid.

11:     Klosko, J.S.; Barlow, D.H.; Tassinari, R.; and Cerny, J.A. A comparison of alprazolam and behavior therapy in treatment of panic disorder. *Journal of Consulting and Clinical Psychology,* 58(1), 77 - 84, 1990.

12:     Barlow and Craske, op cit.

CHAPTER NINE

1:     Ellis, Albert. *How to maintain and enhance your Rational-Emotive Therapy gains.* New York: Institute for Rational-Emotive Therapy, 1984.

2:     Ibid.

172

CHANGING YOUR STINKING THINKING

Prepared by: Ed Nottingham, Ph.D.

C - __Consequences:__ What are the disturbed or inappropriate negative emotions that you felt, e.g., depression, rage, anxiety, panic, strong frustration, etc.?

_____

_____

What were the inappropriate behaviors, those actions that are self-, other-, and/or relationship-defeating?

_____

_____

A - __Activator(s):__ Describe what happened immediately before you started having the feelings and doing the actions described above. The Activator can be actual events as well as feelings or even memories.

_____

_____

B - __Beliefs: Irrational Beliefs__ (iBs) related to the Activator above which cause the emotional and behavior consequences: IBs are rigid, illogical, absolutistic, get in your way of reaching your goals, keep you from fully enjoying life, and generally can't be supported with facts. The principle iB is demandingness, which is reflected in thoughts and statements including musts, shoulds, oughts, got-tos, have tos, and general "musturbation." Four (4) other iBs which stem from "musturbation" include self- and other- damnation (self and other rating), awfulizing (more than 100% bad!), "I-can't-stand-it-itis," and always and never thinking.

_____

_____

    Disputation: Once you've detected your irrational beliefs, it's time to start putting these beliefs and attitudes "on trial" in your psychological court of law. These beliefs are tested by looking for proof and facts to support the attitudes. Use questions (debates) like: Where's the evidence that supports my belief? Where is it written (other than in my personal book of rules)? Can I prove my belief beyond a shadow of a doubt? Is there an universal law (like the law of gravity) that would back up my belief? How is the belief helping me right now and helping me to reach my goals in life? Is my belief logical?

_____

_____

    Effective Beliefs or Effects of Disputing: These are the new **Rational Beliefs (rBs)** that you developed as a result of active, forceful disputing. Rational beliefs are logical, preferential (wanting, wishing, and desiring rather than requiring and demanding), indicate flexible (non-absolutistic) thinking are , self-, other-, and relationship-enhancing, and help us to reach our goals and achieve our purposes in life.

_____

_____

F -   **Feelings** and new behaviors/actions accomplished after successfully disputing and developing new rational beliefs. Remember, after successful debating of irrational beliefs you won't necessarily feel good! The goal is to eliminate inappropriate, negative emotions such as depression, guilt, anger, panic, and intense frustration and replace these with appropriate feelings such as regret, disappointment, sadness, concern, annoyance, etc.

    So, after I finished debating and disputing my irrational beliefs andchanging these to rational beliefs, I changed my unhealthy feelings of _____to_____.

    Before disputing, the old behavior action that was defeating (to me, others, or relationships) was _____ and after I created my new rational belief, the new behavior/action was

_____

_____

_____.

174

RATIONAL OR IRRATIONAL?

Prepared by: Edgar Nottingham, Ph.D.

When is a thought or belief irrational, unhealthy, self-defeating, and maladaptive?

To find out whether it is or not, ask yourself four (4) questions: (From Persons, 1989)

(1)   Does this thought help my mood right now?

(2)   Does this thought help me think productively about the situation?

(3)   Does this thought help me behave and act appropriately and in a healthy way?

(4)   Does this thought make my core **rational beliefs** stronger right now? (Otherwise, the thought is feeding the irrational belief sharks!)

If you answered "**NO**" to any of these questions, there is a good chance that your thinking is irrational.

But, I'm still not sure I understand!   What's the difference between irrational and rational beliefs?   Tell me more about the real difference between irrational and rational beliefs.

Irrational beliefs are: those that are defeating and destructive to self, others, and relationships; are not based on scientific facts; are illogical; would not stand up in a "psychological court of law"; are rigid; and take the form of musts, shoulds, have to's, got to's, need to's, and other forms of "absolutistic" and demanding thinking. Put simply, irrational beliefs are forms of **thinking garbage and are based on bold-faced lies!**

Rational beliefs are: those that are generally help us to reach our goals in life; are enhancing to self, others, and relation-ships; are based on facts; are logical; would stand up in a "psycho-

175

logical court of law"; are flexible; and are based on preferring, wanting, wishing, and desiring "personal rules of living" and philoophies. Rational beliefs are based on **truth**, even though we may not always like the truth.

So, I've got these irrational beliefs or what has been called "stinking thinking. "What do I do now?

Irrational beliefs are changed to **rational beliefs** by using the techniques of challenging, debating, and disputing. We take the belief that we believe to be irrational and put it on trial:

(1)   Is the belief **logical**? Where's the logic for what you believe? Is there an universal law of physics that says that just because we believe something, it **MUST** happen?

(2)   Are there any hard, scientific facts to support your beliefs? (This is called **empiricism**.) Is there any real evidence to support your belief beyond a reasonable doubt? Just because you want something, does that mean that it **ABSOLUTELY** has to be? Are you confusing reasons why you want something to be with thinking that **IT ABSOLUTELY MUST BE**? You can come up with millions of reasons why you want it, but probably not why it must be.

(3)   What about the **practical** value of thinking and believing the way you are? How does thinking the way you are right now help you to reach your goals and to find more happiness in life? What really happens when you believe the irrational beliefs? Is there any long-term benefit to holding on to the belief?

I see. The beliefs are irrational because they are not logical, aren't supported by any facts whatsoever (other than I want it or just think that it SHOULD BE), and are certainly hurting me right now. So, what I am to do? Just not think about it or think about something else?

176

No. Your goal is never "not to think" or to just distract yourself, but to think rationally about the event or other activator that triggered your irrational thinking. Once the irrational beliefs have been put on trial and not supported, you now go from **D** to **E**, or **EFFECTIVE THINKING**. This is where your replace the irrational beliefs with rational attitudes, beliefs, and self-statement. Effective (rational) beliefs, thoughts, and philosophies usually sound like this:

> I wish that had not happened, but it did happen. And, you know what? I can stand it even if I don't like it so much.
>
> Yes, I did fail at something, but I'm not a failure as person. I accept myself unconditionally without having to accept the bad actions or behaviors that I did. Now I can work to change these problem behaviors and actions.
>
> What happened was bad, but not **AWFUL, TERRIBLE,** or **HORRIBLE**. Awful means at least 100 percent bad, and nothing in life can be 100 percent bad.
>
> Yes, he or she did leave me (or treat me badly). While I profoundly wish he (or she) had not done so, it happened! No universal law says that people **MUST** always be the way I want. If they had to, then guess what? They **WOULD**. The fact that the person acted other than how I wish is proof positive that reality is the way it is, and not how I think it **SHOULD BE!**
>
> Life dealt me a bad hand, but I can stand it, and it's not the end of my world!

Now, the next step is to **DO SOME HOMEWORK**. Use the RET Self-Help Form, Changing Your Stinking Thinking Form, or just take a piece of paper and put an A, B, C, D, E, and F on the page. Practice finding your undesirable emotional and behavioral consequences, the activators that triggered the feelings and actions, and the underlying irrational beliefs causing the inappropriate feelings and actions. Next, start disputing the irrational beliefs until you are able to replace the **iBs** with **rBs** and you have created the new appropriate feelings and actions.

INSTRUCTIONS FOR COMPLETION OF THE DAILY MOOD RECORD

It is important to complete the Daily Mood Record at the end of each day. Using this mood record provides a way of measuring changes that take place, based on the self-report of the person completing the record for his or her mood.

The Daily Mood Record is actually eight to 14 scales combined into one record. Emotions (moods) vary along a continuum, base on intensity and also vary vased on whether or not the mood is helpul (appropriate) or unhelpful and unhealthy (inappropriate).

Start with anxiety. The "Anxiety" subscale of the Daily Mood Record actually represents two (2) scales including "concern," which is the appropriate emotion that helps people to accomplish goals, and "anxiety," which tends to interfere with the accomplishment of various tasks. For example, if a student was studying for a test and felt no concern at all, he or she would probably not study and might fail the test. A "mild" to "moderate" level of concern will increase the motivation level. However, when concern crosses over the boundary and becomes anxiety, the anxiety may interfere with studying and could also result in failing the test. On the mood record, 1, 2, 3, and 4 represent **concern** ranging from mild (1) to intense (4). Even intense concern is healthy and helps people to be goal-directed. The 0 to 4 could be thought of as a separate scale of "concern" that ranges from 0 to 99 in intensity. Unhealthy anxiety begins at 6 with this level of anxiety serving to block effective thinking, good problem-solving skills, and general coping skills. The number "6" represents the lowest level of inappropriate anxiety while 10 indicates anxiety of such severity that there is probably almost a constant state of turmoil, distress, nervousness, etc. On the scale, 6 to 10 could be though of as a new scale of anxiety ranging from 101 to 199 or even higher.

The depression scale is next. Depression may be thought of as ranging from sadness (regret, disappointment) which is 0 to 4 on the Daily Mood Record (or 0 to 99 if we think of this as being a separate scale for sadness, regret, or disappointment) to depression, which ranges from 6 to 10 and is the persistent depressed mood usually with other symptoms like loss of interest or pleasure in daily activities, change in appetite, sleep disturbance, weight changes, fatigue, poor concentration, etc. Depression is always based on irrational thinking and is an inappropriate mood state. On the scale, 6 to 10 can be thought of as representing the "depression" scale that ranges from 101 to 199.

Same for frustration and anger. If I am feeling mildly frustrated, I am thinking that I don't like something but I can surely stand it, and my mild and appropriate frustration will vary from absent (0) to only mild (4). When "I-can't-stand-it-itis" begins, frustration becomes self-, other-, and relationship-defeating and moves into the unhealthy range (between 6 to 10). The anger continuum ranges from annoyance, irritation, or aggravation (from 0 to 4, or between 0 to 99 on the healthy scale) to anger and rage (6 to 10 or 101 to 199 or higher on the defeating, unhealthy scale). Anger probably always includes absolutistic, dogmatic, godlike thinking with **shoulding** on self, others, or conditions as well as musturbation ("I must, you must, or life conditions must be the way I want . . .")

The "Other" columns are for people to add specific moods, behaviors, or episodes that are being worked on in therapy and are being monitored. For example, individuals may include the frequency of panic attacks, weight, number of cigarettes smoked each day, number of times the person yells, etc. Remember to have specific, objective measures of the events or conditions.

When therapy begins, moods will most likely be in the unhealthy range (6 to 10) and as progress is made, the intensity will drop into the healthy (1 to 4). Change is gradual, and sudden changes should be looked at carefully. While people do .have occasion "death thoughts" (e.g., "I just wish I wouldn't wake up . .), any thoughts of suicide are significant and should be explored in detail.

DAILY MOOD RECORD

Ed Nottingham, Ph.D.
Clinical Psychologist
Diplomate, Cognitive-Behavior Therapy
American Board of Behavioral Psychology

NAME: _____ DATE:_____

At the end of each day, write down the number that best describes the intensity of each emotion or thought listed below. The number will indicate how you felt that day ON AN AVERAGE. As a guideline, if your feelings are in the 1 to 4 range these moods are usually uncomfortable, negative, and appropriate, e.g., sad, annoyed, concerned, etc. However, feelings in the 6 to 10 range are considered negative and inappropriate (unhealthy, self-defeating), e.g., more intense depression, anxiety, anger, etc. Even occasional thoughts of suicide should be noted and discussed with your therapist(s).

```
            ┌──────Appropriate──────┐      ┌──────Inappropriate──────┐
       0 —   1 —   2 —   3 —    4 —   5 —   6 —    7 —   8 —   9 —   10
      NONE   └── MILD ──┘       └ MODERATE ┘       └── SEVERE ──┘   EXTREME
```

Date	Average Anxiety	Average Depression	Average Frustration	Average Anger	Thoughts About Suicide	Other ____	Other ____	Other ____	Other ____

Based on a form developed by Barlow & Craske, 1989.

COMPLETING THE RET
SELF-HELP FORM

Prepared by Ed Nottingham, Ph.D.

(1) Start by identifying an undesirable, unhealthy emotion you want to change. For example, were you feeling depressed, anxious, angry, or extremely frustrated, not just sad, disappointed, concerned, annoyed, or mildly frustrated?

(2) When you first start completing these forms, pick just one feeling that you want to eliminate. People sometimes want to change their anger, frustration, anxiety, and depression, all at one time and on one form! So, for now, just one undesirable, defeating, unhealthy negative emotion per sheet.

(3) Rate the emotion/feeling (the **ueC**) on the 0 (none) to 10 (extreme) scale, for example, depression (8).

(4) Write down the behaviors or actions (the **UBC**) that go along with the feelings, like withdrawal, throwing things, yelling, drinking, using drugs, etc.

(5) What triggered this emotional episode? What happened? Was it a particular event, or a memory, or a feeling? Be as specific as possible when describing the **Activator**.

(6) Now, find the irrational **Belief** sharks! Remember, musturbation creates anger; awfulizing and a sense of threat creates anxiety; "I-can't-stand-it-itis" creates frustration; and self-downing, a negative view of the future, world, and others creates depression.

(7) Once identified, put the irrational belief on trial by using the active **Disputing** techniques discussed in other handouts. Can you prove it beyond a reasonable doubt? Where is the evidence? Is the belief helping you?

(8) When you have not been able to prove your irrational beliefs, then you replace them with rational beliefs at **E**. Demandingness becomes preferring, self-downing becomes self-acceptance, I can't stand it becomes **I CAN STAND IT**, and awfulizing becomes "It's bad but not 100 percent awful!"

(9) Once you have successfully disputed, you will notice a change in your emotions. Depression will lessen and become regret, sadness, disappointment, etc. Inappropriate emotions become negative and appropriate such as concern, mild frustration, and annoyance. If strong feelings such as depression, anger, frustration, and anxiety are still present, then that's a signal that "stinking thinking" is still there. Go back to **B** and look for the underlying irrational beliefs.

(10) "Good thinking gets good results," and as you apply your rational thinking to this and other situations, you will be better able to reach your specific goals.

RET FORM #2

NAME: _____ DATE:_____

Consequences:
    ueC (Undesirable emotional consequences):_____

_____
    ubC (Undesirable behavioral consequences/actions):

_____

Activator:_____

Beliefs: irrational beliefs are:_____

_____.

Disputation (Debate and challenge the identified irrational beliefs):
    (Remember debating requires putting the belief "on trial." Where is the evidence to support the beliefs? Can you **PROVE IT?** Is the thinking helping you feel and act better and in a healthier way? Are you telling yourself factual truths, or a bunch of defeating garbage and lies? Use factual, practical, logical forms of disputing.)

_____
_____.

Effective beliefs (or enhancing new rational beliefs that you have
    created after effective debating and debunking the irration-
    al beliefs):_____

    _____

Feelings (that go along with rational beliefs):_____

_____
_____

Goals you can now achieve using rational thinking:_____

_____.

RET SELF-HELP FORM

Institute for Rational-Emotive Therapy
45 East 65th Street, New York, N.Y. 10021
(212) 535-0822

(A) ACTIVATING EVENTS, thoughts, or feelings that happened just before I felt emotionally disturbed or acted self-defeatingly: _____

(C) CONSEQUENCE or CONDITION—disturbed feeling or self-defeating behavior—that I produced and would like to change: _____

(B) BELIEFS—Irrational BELIEFS (IBs) leading to my CONSEQUENCE (emotional disturbance or self-defeating behavior). Circle all that apply to these ACTIVATING EVENTS (A).	(D) DISPUTES for each circled IRRATIONAL BELIEF. *Examples:* "Why MUST I do very well?" "Where is it written that I am a BAD PERSON?" "Where is the evidence that I MUST be approved or accepted?"	(E) EFFECTIVE RATIONAL BELIEFS (RBs) to replace my IRRATIONAL BELIEFS (IBs). *Examples:* "I'd PREFER to do very well but I don't HAVE TO." "I am a PERSON WHO acted badly, not a BAD PERSON." "There is no evidence that I HAVE TO be approved, though I would LIKE to be."
1. I MUST do well or very well!		
2. I am a BAD OR WORTHLESS PERSON when I act weakly or stupidly.		
3. I MUST be approved or accepted by people I find important!		
4. I NEED to be loved by someone who matters to me a lot!		
5. I am a BAD, UNLOVABLE PERSON if I get rejected.		
6. People MUST treat me fairly and give me what I NEED!		

184

7. People MUST live up to my expectations or it is TERRIBLE!		
8. People who act immorally are undeserving, ROTTEN PEOPLE!		
9. I CAN'T STAND really bad things or very difficult people!		
10. My life MUST have few major hassles or troubles.		
11. It's AWFUL or HORRIBLE when major things don't go my way!		
12. I CAN'T STAND IT when life is really unfair!		
13. I NEED a good deal of immediate gratification and HAVE to feel miserable when I don't get it!		
Additional Irrational Beliefs:		

(F) FEELINGS and BEHAVIORS I experienced after arriving at my EFFECTIVE RATIONAL BELIEFS: _____

I WILL WORK HARD TO REPEAT MY EFFECTIVE RATIONAL BELIEFS FORCEFULLY TO MYSELF ON MANY OCCASIONS SO THAT I CAN MAKE MYSELF LESS DISTURBED NOW AND ACT LESS SELF-DEFEATINGLY IN THE FUTURE.

Joyce Sichel, Ph.D. and Albert Ellis, Ph.D.
Reprinted by permission.

About the Author

Ed Nottingham, Ph.D., (M.S. & Ph.D. in Clinical Psychology, Virginia Polytechnic Institute and State University) is a licensed clinical psychologist in Tennessee and Mississippi and a licensed marital and family therapist in Tennessee. He is a Diplomate in Behavioral and Clinical Psychology of the American Board of Professional (ABPP) and is listed in the National Register of Health Service Providers in Psychology. He is an Associate Fellow and Approved Supervisor in Rational-Emotive Therapy. He is also a Certified Rational Recovery Specialist, Rational Recovery Systems, and is a Clinical Member of the American Association for Marriage and Family Therapy and the American Group Psychotherapy Association.

Professional responsibilities include serving as Clinical Director and a Senior Partner, Germantown Psychological Associates, P.C. He holds (or has held) faculty appointments at Memphis State University (Adjunct - Department of Psychology), University of Mississippi (Adjunct Associate Professor - Department of Psychology), and University of Tennessee Center for the Health Sciences (Clinical Assistant Professor - Department of Psychiatry, Division of Clinical Psychology). He has held offices with various professional associations including the Tennessee Psychological Association and the Memphis Area Psychological Association.